DIM SUM
(Little Pieces of Heart)

•

British Chinese short stories

DIM SUM
(Little Pieces of Heart)

crocus

DIM SUM (Little Pieces of Heart)
British Chinese short stories

First published by Crocus 1997

Crocus Books are published by
Commonword Limited
Cheetwood House, 21 Newton Street,
Manchester. M1 1FZ.

Typeset in Caslon 11/13 point by Justin Larner.
Printed by RAM, Kingsway Park Close,
Kingsway Industrial Park, Derby. DE22 3FT.
Cover design by Verso Design Ltd,
Rutland House, 18 Hilton Street, Manchester. M1 1FR.

Commonword gratefully acknowledges financial assistance from
Association of Greater Manchester Authorities, North West Arts Board
and Manchester City Council.

Crocus Books are distributed by Password (Books) Ltd,
23 New Mount Street, Manchester M4 4DE.

British Library Cataloguing-in-Publication Data. A catalogue
record for this is available from the British Library.

Publisher's Note

We would like to extend our thanks to the following people and organisations for their help in bringing this book to fruition:

Justin Larner
Kwong Lee
Fiona Pymont
Tang Lin
David Tse
Jan Whalen

British Chinese Artists' Association
Manchester Central Library Services
Si Yu Times

Contents

Introduction

Firstly, congratulations to Commonword. This anthology is a long-awaited initiative and offers a welcome chance to sample a selection of delights from the British Chinese selection of the literature trolley. *Dim Sum* presents the work of new talented voices whose stories allow an insight into the experiences of a generation caught between the face of tradition and the development of its own cultural awareness. Further and above this, *Dim Sum* offers the reader an entertaining and thoroughly engaging read. Like the snack-sized bites (literally 'little pieces of heart') to which the title of the anthology refers, *Dim Sum* will leave you craving for more. There are fifteen stories to choose from, put together through a unique and clever stir-fry.

The scope of the compilation encompasses the work of eleven writers working either from personal experience or a distinctly British Chinese perspective. The burning question featured within many of the stories is a timely one of relation and self – that of being both British and of Chinese descent and the often problematic nature of establishing a coherent identity against this.

To take just three stories, *Discovery* by Graham Chan is a keenly observed and honest portrait of the assimilation of British attitudes by two brothers who have taken different life paths and is, perhaps, the most apt story in *Dim Sum* to parallel issues of cultural dilemmas.

Told in an accomplished manner at once subtle and lyrical, *Daydream of a Butterfly* by K. P. William Cheng expertly unfolds the somewhat sterile existence of a man as he works yet another day of his life away at the office, a monotony disrupted only by his tendency to deliberate on his position in the world and observations of others.

Approaching British Chinese kitsch, Hi Ching constructs

an entire new genre with a very playful pen. The innovative and off-beat *Violin Practice* tells the story of a boy forbidden to attend a pop concert by his parents. From this misleadingly modest premise, the story escalates into heights of absurd mayhem and frenzy as the repressed Huang exacts an imaginative revenge on the parents.

I feel that *Dim Sum* is a truly unique book in that it speaks to me directly with a British Chinese voice. But as refreshing as it is to see writing emerging from a cultural context that I happen to share, I am also certain that a diversity of readers will easily enjoy the work. Without pushing food analogies too far, a compliment should be handed to the subtleties of flavour that the collection contains as a whole, and I suggest that there is room for a main course to be served up by each writer in future.

Roll on the Banquet!

Andy-Gunn Yu Cheung
*British Chinese Artists' Association

* The British Chinese Artists' Association (BCAA) is a non-profit making organisation that exists to increase public awareness and education in Chinese arts through the promotion, support and development of both traditional and contemporary work. Tele : 0171 267 6133.

Little Rabbit

Tai Lai Kwan

Oh! The pain.

Ah Beng moved his lumpish limbs warily as he got ready for work. His joints creaked and yelled out in protest at every movement. The afternoon nap had not helped at all. He had the dream again. In the dream (it was always the same dream), Mei Kuei was drifting away from him in the water. He increased his effort – he had never been a strong swimmer, but now his movements were smooth, strong and rhythmic. Mei Kuei turned round and besought him with her eyes. Just a few more strokes and he would reach her. Then a dead body floated across his path. He pushed away from it in disgust and frustration. Now he was further away from Mei Kuei again. Something else was dragging at his feet. He struggled hard… It was always at this point that he awoke. One day, one day he would reach her and they would start their life again as they had vowed. *Would this be the day?*

Years of futile searching had not dimmed his hope. He knew the Lord of the Nether World was exacting his price. So be it. *Less and less hair, and greyer by the day. Would she still recognise…* Even before the thought could take full shape, Ah Beng thrust it aside guiltily. Of course she would recognise him. How dare he doubt her.

The dreary room stared back at him through the reflection in the mirror. It was a spartan and claustrophobic room, relieved only by a small porthole-like window near the ceiling to one side. A single bed laid squashed underneath, the mattress on it worn so thin he might as well have been sleeping on loose springs. A single door wardrobe with a gaping hole where its handle used to be stood next to it. Peeling wallpaper, blackened with age to a mouldy brown added to the air of

1

despondency. *This would not do for Mei Kuei. Oh, Ah Beng, Ah Beng. You miserable…*

Ah Beng shuffled quickly out of the room, locking his despair behind.

•

'Stop day dreaming, pig-head Beng! And move that fat arse of yours!'

Ah Beng had barely changed into his uniform before 'goldfish eyes' tore into him. Still panting from climbing the stairs, he shuffled silently to take up his position, quite oblivious to his boss's derision. A little abuse like this could hardly perturb him – if the sky should fall, use it as a blanket – wasn't that what grandma Mu always said? No, there was only one thing Ah Beng cared about passionately, his one mission in life: finding Mei Kuei, his little rabbit.

He had only started work here a week ago. He was lucky to find work so soon after hitting town. It was thanks to Old Chung, an old comrade in arms he worked with years ago in another town. They were both itinerant workmen, living from hand to mouth, lonely souls seemingly destined to whittle away their hours in run-down lodges masquerading as B & Bs.

The restaurant was busy that night. It was a large room. But as with a lot of Chinese restaurants, there was no feeling of space, only the closeness of bodies as diners were crammed together to squeeze in just that one more table. Loud hoots of laughter and banter were coming from table four. Tucked in the far corner, the racket still pierced through the general din of the restaurant. Ah Beng looked towards the corner. The smoke from cigarettes and steaming-hot dishes combined with the multitude of bodies obscured his vision. He could roughly make out five punk-looking youths having a riot of a time, almost flaunting their bad behaviour, as if challenging any one to dare stop them.

'They've been at it all afternoon. The boys are connected with the Triad, you know. Thank goodness they've asked for the bill.' Old Chung, noticing Ah Beng's glance, said to him, 'Hey, listen, can you get the next dish for table three, I've got to make a dash for the toilet.'

'Sure, no problem.' Ah Beng smiled to himself. Old Chung thought nobody noticed, but everyone was wise to his tricks. They all called him three-toilet Chung. Every shift he would make at least three nature calls, loading his share of the work onto others. But he was a cheery old man, so most of them, especially Ah Beng, never minded.

As usual, Ah Beng tried to scan the female guests as he made his way around. The steam from the sizzling beef in special sauce tickled his nose. He squinted his eyes, bit his mouth and screwed up his nose, trying hard not to sneeze. It was almost with a sigh of relief that he laid down the plate for table three. One more second and he would have spattered his own special sauce onto the dish.

The group of rowdy young thugs were leaving. They brushed passed Ah Beng roughly, nearly causing him to lose his balance. He turned round, but only in time to see their backs. The group was swaggering their way through the tables. A young man in a black jacket with one arm around his girl brought up the rear. Ah Beng caught sight of the purple tips of the girl's hair and thought to himself, 'If my daughter looked and behaved like that, I'd kick her out of the house. My little rabbit is so different.'

He felt warm all over as he thought of his little rabbit. Mei Kuei was not what you would call pretty. But she was so full of life. There was always a twinkle in her eye. The twinkles that said, 'I love you' to him in every glance. Every time she was puzzled or angry, she would bite her two front teeth hard on her lower lip. Those little teeth that stuck out just that little bit – that was why he called her his little rabbit.

'Come on Ah Beng, enough of your day dreaming. Coming to the casino?' Old Chung slapped him hard across the back and chuckled.

Ah Beng wasn't keen on gambling. But he needed to visit places where people gathered, because where there were people, there was a chance he could find his little rabbit.

The casino was even noisier and smokier than the restaurant. Ah Beng stood behind Old Chung at the mahjong table, ostensibly to keep him company, but his eyes were roving through the crowd, searching for his illusive dream. *Oh little rabbit, where are you! Goddess of Mercy, pray help me find her.*

All of Chinatown's restaurant workers could be found in casinos after work. There was precious little entertainment for these people who kept such alien hours compared to the rest of the population. Bodies were standing three or four deep round various gambling tables. Tempers were short. Often squeezing turned into shoving. Curses and abusive language were everywhere. Lady luck was not too generous that night. Among the sweating, swearing throng, Ah Beng passed his gaze over all the Chinese female faces. Nothing else registered in his senses. Lingering, pondering over each face, he dared not skip over any single feature for fear of missing Mei Kuei in his haste. He was destined to be disappointed that night.

Sleep never came easily to him. His mind was too full of the past. If only the war had not reached them. For the zillionth time, he relived the many happy moments Mei Kuei shared with him – especially the times they spent working in the field side by side. She loved to play tricks on him, little harmless tricks, like slipping a handful of mud down the back of his collar; sprinkling him with water when he was not looking; once she even hid a little field mouse in his knapsack.

Then their village too was swamped by the war.

Overnight it was as if the gods had all gone into hiding. Nobody could work in the field any more. Even children as young as ten years old were carrying guns, not just playing at soldiers, but taking part in senseless killing in the name of the… what? He could never understand just what it was they were supposed to be fighting for – he just knew that when the men in uniform came out of the jungle, the villagers had better obey every command or it would not be just their own lives they lost but those of their families as well. In spite of everything, he was quite willing to carry on; after all, who would look after grandma Mu if he went away? But Mei Kuei would not hear of it. No, they must escape. After all, didn't second uncle send word from the city that he could help them? It was Ah Beng who capitulated in the end. As usual, he could never say no to his little rabbit. *Ah, Mei Kuei, my little rabbit, if only I had been more firm at the time.*

Weeks went by. Ah Beng settled into his routine in the restaurant. Old Chung told him those young triad thugs were often around, but luckily not in their shifts. Old Chung did not approve of troublemakers like them, and Ah Beng agreed with him.

'Not our night tonight. Those young thugs are here. I hate the sight of them. Would you mind serving the last dish for me?' Old Chung got hold of him the minute he emerged from the changing room to start his shift.

Ah Beng nodded and smiled resignedly. Old Chung knew he was a soft touch.

The young thugs were up to their usual caterwauling tricks. Ah Beng had to move in carefully among the flailing arms with cigarettes sticking out at all angles while their owners boasted of some adventures or other. And then he saw her. The shock was so great, he just put down the dish, turned and walked back towards the kitchen.

The girl was one of the young punks he had espied earlier. The one he thought he would kick out if she was his daughter! Her hair was cut short and spiky, with an orange streak down one side, purple down another, and she had far too much make up on for her age. In spite of all these changes, Ah Beng still recognised her at once – how could he do otherwise – this face, whose features were burnt into every pore of his being, the face that he had been searching for every single waking moment of his life. Especially those teeth! Those little rabbit teeth! And the way she screwed up her pert little nose at the young man sitting next to her just now; why, that was exactly how Mei Kuei always looked at him whenever she was teasing. *Little rabbit! Little rabbit!*

They were on a boat. No, that was not a boat. That was a death hole. You could smell death, together with vomit, urine and faeces. The bodies were crammed every which way. You couldn't tuck a piece of paper in edgewise. There was a constant droning in the air, a cacophony of moans, whimpering and spluttering of the multitude of suffering humanity. But he was happy. Mei Kuei was lying in his arms. Gingerly, he brushed aside a wisp of hair which had fallen across her cheek – if one could call those sunken hollows cheeks. Thirty three days. It did not sound very long. Yet the sickness that swept through the cabin had struck down his little rabbit. As he held her now bony hands in his, he closed his eyes to call up the image of the robust, cheeky playmate he knew. The memory of Mei Kuei laughing and full of life proved too much for him. He brushed aside his tears and opened his eyes.

Ah Beng glanced down at the body, now barely breathing in his arms. Soon, it would be all over, and they could start again in their next life. Yes, they had made their vows. As the days passed and it became impossible to pretend otherwise, they pledged themselves to each other anew. Ah Beng felt at ease. His hand strayed to the little army knife taped to his body inside his waist band; comforted that it was still there, secured. He would follow Mei Kuei the instant she left on her journey to the Nether World. When they reached the bridge at the gate of the Nether World, they would not drink the soup-of-forgetfulness offered by the old lady who guarded the bridge. They would come through the wheel of rebirth, remembering their love and their vows. The Goddess of Mercy would be kind to them, seeing that they had suffered so in this life. There would be a terrible price to pay for refusing the soup-of-forgetfulness, of course. But they would bear it. They had vowed that come what may, they would be together in the next life. Oh yes, little rabbit...

'Ah Beng, for goodness sake, what's wrong with you tonight...?'

Ah Beng looked up, dazed. What's this place? Who's this man with the bulging big eyes shouting at him? Ah Beng could see his mouth opening and closing like a goldfish gulping for air, but his words were coming at him through a thick mist. Ah Beng shook his head in an effort to clear his mind – but the only words echoing around in there seemed to be 'little rabbit'. Of course! Little rabbit. He'd found her! Now they could live happily ever after like they planned. And to think he was actually cursing the Goddess of Mercy the other day. What a sinner. He must make amends. He would bring Mei Kuei to the... *Oh no, they were paying the bills!*

Ah Beng swung round. There she was. The group was at the top of the stairs, still bandying about. The young man in the black jacket, as usual, had one arm about her waist.

'Mei Kuei!'

Ah Beng rushed over and pulled her towards him. Surprised, the girl tried to break free, but Ah Beng was holding onto her tight. His one eye wild, his cheeks flushed with excitement, he was almost incoherent: 'It's me, it's me, little rabbit, it's me! Thank the sky and the earth! I've finally found you. Don't look at me like that, I'm your handsome sweetheart, you always called me that, remember? Please say you remember... please don't tease, Mei Kuei, not now... please...'

'Ha-ha-ha-ha!' Uncontrollable mirth broke out among the group, drowning out Ah Beng's feverish attempt to get through to Mei Kuei. The young man in the black jacket managed to stifle his guffaw long enough to ask, 'You know this man, Cindy?'

'What, this one-eyed pig face? You insult my taste! He's probably some dirty old man high on his last porno. Hey fatso, go wank yourself off on somebody else.' The girl looked at Ah Beng with undisguised contempt and loathing.

'You heard her, fat arse. Go look yourself in the mirror... handsome sweetheart... ha! What does that make me? Mr. Universe?' The young man brought his fist down hard on Ah Beng's arm. The sharp pain forced Ah Beng to drop back.

'What happened, Ah Beng? What's going on?' Old Chung noticed the commotion and rushed over.

But Ah Beng wasn't listening. He wasn't even aware of the pain in his arm or that Old Chung was trying hard to hold him steady. All he could see were those eyes — so cruel, so much contempt, so far removed from the loving glances that he had carried in his memory all these years. And that smirk! She had bowed under the threats of the Lord of the Nether World and taken the soup of forgetfulness.

Tears came gushing down Ah Beng's cheeks. He felt his knees slowly giving way under him. As he collapsed onto the floor, he could still hear the laughter drifting up from the stairs: 'Hey little rabbit, handsome sweetheart wants you... tsk... tsk... tsk... rabbit, rabbit...!'

Daydream of a Butterfly

Paul Wong

It's another day. I wake up sweaty from the nightmares I've been having. The duvet peels off my body like the skin of a banana. I sit up and remove the mouthguard that stops me from grinding my teeth to little yellow stubs. I've been chewing the plastic crescent all night, it flops out of my mouth, opaque and covered in saliva like some kind of dead baby alien. Next, I take out the similarly colourless rubber strip that holds my nostrils apart, stopping me snoring, and preventing the build-up of bad breath bacteria in my mouth. The device bounces out of my nostrils and I pinch my nose tightly to make sure it doesn't explode into the flat nub of flesh with two gaping holes, so beloved of cartoonists when they draw the noses of Chinese people. I swirl my tongue around my liberated mouth and feel sore craters in my gums, mouth ulcers stinging and burning away at my bubble-gum flesh.

●

It's time to get ready and I swing my legs out of the bed and slip my feet into a pair of flip-flops. These white bits of flat rubber with blue thongs do make me look like a beggar in Kowloon, but I think it's more important to have well-aired, non-fungal, verrucae-free feet than be a victim to fashion. Anyway, no-one else ever sees them. I flip-flop my way to the bathroom, perform my various well-rehearsed ablutions: my excretions are examined, my teeth, brushed, flossed and slooshed with mouthwash and my body is bathed and moisturised with a whole variety of vitamin E, aloe vera, evening primrose oil and coconut butter products. Now I'm ready for my clothes, I'm conscious of what impression I want to make this morning. My mother's advice resonates in my mind : 'Always make a good impression, remember you have

9

to be twice as good as anyone else to make a success of yourself in this foreign land. People will always judge you by the way you look.'

•

Returning to my bedroom, I open the wardrobe and choose a lightweight grey suit, a white shirt with a button-down collar and a silver-grey tie with a red swirl on it. I also pull out some black cotton boxer shorts and black socks from a half-open drawer. The outfit goes on methodically: boxer shorts first, then socks followed by the shirt, then the trousers then the tie and finally the jacket. In my socks, I pad back up the corridor and examine myself in the bathroom mirror. I look older today. My hair is thinning and the wrinkles on my face, even though it's still puffy with sleep, seem to be connecting to make up some kind of road map. Everyone says I still look young for my age. 'Your skin is so elastic and your hair is so jet-black. You look half your age. That's the wonder of being Oriental,' say all these wrinkled-and-grey-haired-by-thirty friends of mine. But what they don't seem to realise is that it's not so simple. Okay we do seem to stay younger looking for longer, but as soon as we start to show those tell-tale signs of entropy, our bodies go for it big time: the famed and envied elastic skin turns almost overnight into a baggy wrinkled covering of old leather, our hair whitens and drops and we swiftly shrink down to the hobbling miniature statures of our grandparents.

•

I tear myself away from the mirror and head for the kitchen to prepare myself some breakfast. The sun streams in through the kitchen window and it looks like it's going to be another scorching summer's day – all those carcinogenic rays of sunshine sparking off melanomas and making the air even more difficult to breathe than usual. Opening the fridge, I take out some of the special dumplings my mother sent me and pop them into a shiny metal steamer. These little pyramids of sticky rice and meat are deliciously addictive and I've eschewed my usual bowel-churning blend of muesli, banana and bran to relish these culinary gifts from my mother. As the steamer huffs and puffs I pour myself some orange juice and lay out my cocktail of 'dietary supplements': megamultivitamins, Starflower oil capsules, ginseng tablets, a phial of Royal Jelly, Cod Liver Oil capsules and a variety of minerals to keep my body balanced. I gulp them down one by one and then take out the hot rice pyramids in their green jackets of bamboo leaves from the steamer. The dumplings were created to celebrate the self-sacrificial heroism of a Chinese General who threw himself in a river. I think about the irony of being posthumously honoured by a pyramid of sticky rice as I strip one of them of its leafy skin, dip it into some chilli and garlic sauce and take a bite into its warm flesh.

•

After three of the dumplings I brush my teeth again, organise my briefcase and put on my black brogues, double-knotting the laces. I take my keys from the hook by the door and out I go. It takes me twenty minutes to get to my office and before I know it I'm at my workstation yet again, powering up my computer, hearing its familiar buzz and seeing the 'message waiting' light flash on my phone. As the morning goes by I daydream of another life: of donning a leather jacket and fedora and being an adventurer around the globe: 'Indiana Chong and the Sacred Sword of Shiva'; of saving the world from recklessly evil megalomaniacs: 'My name's Chong, James Chong of Her Majesty's Secret Service'; of a whole library of fantasy lives. I stare at my computer screen as I type another letter, another report and in the part of me that's always too conscious, always too aware, I see my life ebbing away eventlessly.

•

My colleagues seem to have no problems with obscurity and mediocrity. One secretary, Kate always seems happy and cheery, she's a walking advert for simplicity and uncomplication. Normally she wears t-shirts five times too small for her and sprayed-on satin or PVC trousers but today she's got on a bright blue cheong sam: a traditional Chinese dress made of shiny satin with intricate embroidered flowers and butterflies on it. Kate's 36D breasts (I asked her what her bra size was when I was very drunk at last year's Christmas party) push against the material and I can see the flabby flesh around her armpits ooze over her bra-strap under the dress. The cheong sam is much too small for Kate's large Caucasian frame and I can see she has trouble walking and moving in it. She sees me eyeing her and mistakes my critical gaze for a lusty leer and self-consciously tries to straighten out the cheong sam, which keeps riding up her body. She pulls the hem of the dress downwards to get rid of the tyres of material forming around her body. It's all too much for the knotted buttons and cheap stitching of the dress and there's a series of rips and unbuttonings which reveal more of Kate than even she would like. She runs off to the ladies' toilet embarrassed and as I watch her teetering on her platform sandals I remember reading somewhere that the reason why Chinese men liked foot-binding women was that it made the women look helpless when they tried to walk on their crippled feet.

•

At lunchtime I break off from the usual exodus to the nearby sandwich bar and decide to treat myself to a meal from the nearby Chinese restaurant: The Jade Garden. These occasional lunchtime visits to my culinary roots do a wonder for me. As I sweat over a plate of mixed seafood and rice swathed in bright orange chilli sauce calligraphy, I feel myself again. It's like a sudden epiphany each time I taste the monosodium glutamate in the food and I am reborn and renewed with every mouthful of rice or noodles. I sip the jasmine tea and use my handkerchief to wipe the sweat from my brow. I look at the waiter, sitting by a rotary fan reading a Chinese newspaper scruffily dressed in the standard outfit of white shirt, black trousers and black bowtie. I wonder what he's thinking and I try to read the front page of the newspaper but my Chinese is so rusty I can only make out a few characters in the headlines.

•

As a riposte to the waiter I unfurl my copy of *The Guardian* and read about various horrors around the world, sighing deeply at all the civil wars, environmental pollution, religious intolerances and human rights abuses between each sip of my tea. I force myself to read every article. I feel impotent and useless. I wonder how I can help, how I can make a difference. My mother says it's all fate, my father tells me to look after myself and forget all this 'wanting to be a hero business'. I look over at the waiter and he seems content, living from day to day, working, eating, sleeping. Why isn't that enough for me? Where am I going in my life? I've always heard how the Chinese have produced such great philosophers, but all I do is keep asking questions but not finding any answers. I drain the last of my tea and look at the residue, the black bits of tea at the bottom of the small cup. I look for a message, a sign, but see only something resembling a badly constructed stick insect. I swirl the cup's contents again and look even closer at the pattern made by the dried tea leaves. It's a butterfly.

•

I leave the restaurant and make my way back to work, worrying about all the pollution I'm breathing in. I've got a chilli sauce stain on my tie that almost, but not quite, blends in with the tie's red design. With my stomach full, I think about food, how important it is, how my family life has always revolved around it. My first memories are of being fed, of being stuffed to the brim with food I didn't want; my mother's heavily pancaked face leering over me with something wriggling in the grip of a pair of slippery plastic chopsticks and my father hiccuping in the background and turning a vicious shade of red as he takes another sip of brandy 'to cure his cold'. It's funny how Chinese physiology handles alcohol so badly, our faces light up like prostitute's light bulbs telling everyone that we've been drinking.

·

In the reception of my office I pass Kate who's now dressed in a borrowed baggy cream t-shirt and someone's spare pair of grey track-suit bottoms. I smile at her as she hurries past me, her cheeks red with over-working blood vessels. Once again Kate sparks off a memory: of finding the phrase 'Chinese Blush' in some lexicon of erotic terms that was being passed around amongst a sex-obsessed circle of adolescent schoolboys, of which I was a member. 'Chinese Blush: used to describe the reddening of the cheeks and erogenous zones after orgasm'. I breathe in the trail of scent that Kate has left in her wake and feel faintly aroused.

·

Back at my desk, I make a call to my parents whilst the rest of my colleagues are busy gossiping and catching up on what's been happening in various television soaps. My mother answers the phone, her voice is as heavily accented as ever but after the initial sense of talking to a complete foreigner, my ears adapt and her voice develops a warm clarity: she's dear old mum again. We speak for a while about what I've been doing, what new scandal my sister is up to and my father's heart condition. I press her to talk about herself but, as usual, she neatly side-steps herself, her feelings and her health, while still managing to make me feel guilty for not caring enough. My father growls into earshot and I speak with him, his lazy sentence construction made worse by his playing up of his 'dodgy ticker' and taking long pauses in-between words. He asks me about the Masters degree course I never took and whether I have enough money. I feign being called back to work and wind-up the conversation, my father hangs up abruptly and although this is just his way it still makes me feel as if he doesn't give a damn about me.

·

14

The rest of the day waddles by, I clear my work-load, play a computer game given to me by one of my PC-symbiote cousins and phone my sister, Christina. We joke about our dysfunctional family and she tells me how she's thinking of dropping out of her pharmacy course and becoming a circus performer or actress or singer. These new vocational interests have been inspired by her latest boyfriend: an all-singing, all-dancing acrobat actor whom she met at a party a few months ago. Christina's had a whole rainbow of male companions and each one has managed to disappoint me in some way, either they lack intelligence or looks or something. Although she's had boyfriends of different races and mixes she's never picked a Chinese guy to go out with. She told me that she isn't sexually attracted to any of the Chinese men she's ever met, they didn't have any personality or style she said, and if they did they were most likely gay. Christina's current beau is of South American descent, with a big nose, long curly hair and a muscular 'toast rack' stomach: she describes him to me as if he were a new car. She sounds laid-back about it all but there's a fear deep down in her voice, an unspoken worry that she's only being used again, that this boyfriend, like nearly all the rest, has a fixed idea about who she is and perhaps is just temporarily indulging his fetish for 'China Dolls'.

.

I worry for my sister, time and time again she falls for the same lines, the same sense of excitement and novelty that each guy offers at the beginning but which wanes as the terms of the relationship become clearer and one or other party gets scared or bored. She herself is scared of settling down, of committing to one person. Marriage as we've been brought up to see it, is for good, the commitment you make to family is unshakeable and permanent, for better or for worse. I remember holding Christina in my arms as our parents fought in the next room, listening to the crash of objects being hurled and of screams and shouts as blows and scratches were exchanged. We would pray for the fighting to end and each time when everything seemed irreconcilable, the following morning we'd find my parents together at the breakfast table, holding the family together, painfully pretending that everything was normal.

•

I tell Christina to take care and to contact me soon. I finish off the rest of the work I have to do on automatic pilot, immersed in my day-dreaming. The end of my working day comes and I go for a quick pint of Guinness with a few colleagues from work. I tease Kate about her impromptu striptease and she blushes and blows cigarette smoke into my face, knowing my loathing of passive smoking. As I turn away from Kate and try to cough discretely someone nudges me and whispers that blowing cigarette smoke in someone's face is a come-on: an invitation to try it on, to make a pass. I shake my head and throw out the gossipy notion that Kate might fancy me. It's still hot and light outside and as we all stand outside the pub overheating, I smell my own body odour mix with Kate's perfume. I volunteer to buy another round of drinks, a few people decline my offer and leave for home and I go into the pub with a twenty pound note in my hand trying to remember who wanted which drink. Kate offers to give me a hand and I hear the boys from the office whoop and make the most of the double entendre as Kate follows me in.

•

At the bar, Kate smiles at me and says that it is a shame that her dress ripped, I agree and suggest she could get it mended or buy a new one. She tells me that she bought it from a really expensive and trendy shop, she tells me how the Oriental look is really fashionable at the moment. I'm shocked when she tells me how much she paid for the dress and tell her that I'm sure I could get something similar a lot cheaper from some of the shops in Chinatown or even from some of my relatives in Hong Kong. I'm just being pragmatic but Kate takes this as a grand gesture of help and friendship and begins to flirtatiously remind me that I already know one set of her measurements and says that I'll have to measure the rest of her for the dress. I blush and then I'm saved by the barman asking me for my order. I fluster through some further conversation with Kate, about where she lives, her flatmates, her surprisingly ambitious aspirations and her modest roots in an estate in South East London. The drinks line up on the plastic draining trays on the bar and Kate tells me how she has always been fascinated by Oriental things and thinks the current vogue for the Suzy Wong-look is wonderful. She asks me if I think the fringed bob hairstyle that goes with the Chinese-tart-with-a-heart image would suit her. I smile and tell her I think she looks lovely just as she is and hand her two full pint glasses to take outside.

•

By the time twilight begins to fall, I've switched to drinking lager and I'm on my fourth pint. I can already feel my cheeks getting hotter and redder and my head feels light and loose. I also feel a little claustrophobic jammed against the wall of the pub with Kate leaning increasingly into me as she ploughs her way through her sixth spritzer. Worrying about my liver, I decide to leave my beer unfinished. Kate rattles the ice in her glass and asks if I've got a girlfriend yet. I shrug and deliver the standard reply of not having found 'Miss Right' and Kate presses into my right shoulder even more. My other colleagues are talking about some sporting scandal and the latest movies in town. I think how banal it all sounds and reflect on the events I read about earlier. I look at the darkening sky and shiver. Kate pats me on the lapel of my suit and asks if I'm okay and I tell her that twilight always makes me feel low and a little depressed. She pouts and reassures me that everything will be alright in a half-sincere and half-patronising tone of voice. I grab my briefcase and make a move to leave, Kate seems a bit surprised and I hold her arm reassuringly and tell her that I'm not feeling very well but that we'll arrange a time for a dress-fitting soon. She smiles and then is distracted by someone offering her another drink.

•

Back at my apartment I strip off my clothes and go to the toilet to relieve my overstretched bladder. Afterwards, I stand in front of the bathroom mirror, looking at my naked body, my soft hairless skin and unmuscular flesh. I raise my arms as if to surrender to someone on the other side of the mirror, crucifying my reflection. I scream a silent scream, stretching my mouth to its furthest extent. My hands drop once again to my sides and I put on a pair of black shorts and a white t-shirt that were hanging on the back of the bathroom door. I go to the front room and open the main window and lean out to look onto the road where I live. I'm on the third floor of my building and as I lean out I can see the sun bleeding out on the horizon of roofs on the buildings opposite mine and night begins to take over. Suddenly, out of nowhere a butterfly flies straight at me, swerves at my face and lands on my right shoulder. I can feel its tiny legs through the thin cotton sleeve of my t-shirt. I slowly strain my head around to look at my shoulder. The butterfly looks like a tropical variety, with large shimmering velvety wings of bright purple, several shades of brown, and circular patches of white. It performs a little circular dance, opening and closing its wings and finally settles with its head towards mine. Its wings open to reveal its exotic pattern against the white cotton fabric. The butterfly is motionless now and I turn my head slowly once again to look at the sky and watch the stars appear.

Old Partner

Tai Lai Kwan

One of her teardrops fell on Uncle Ming's face. Tenderly, she wiped it off with her fingers. He looked rather serene, lying there. Yet Aunty Ming couldn't help noticing the slight frown on his forehead. 'Why didn't you tell me? You must have known something's wrong. How could you not let me share your last days? Forgive me old partner. I know you'd still be with me if I'd been around.' The wave of pain overwhelmed her again. Aunty Ming felt herself going faint. She clung onto the side of the coffin, wishing she too, could lie in there with her husband.

'Come on, Ma. Come sit down here for a while. You must be exhausted after the long journey.' Ah Wai gently led his mother to a chair on the side. Silently, he put a cup of tea in her hands. Aunty Ming looked up at her son. No, it was not his fault. She blamed herself. She should never have gone to Manchester.

The village monks had started on their prayers to the dead: a symphony of murmuring interspersed with bells and cymbals filled the air. The rhythmic intonation, combined with spiralling smoke from the incense gave her a drugged feeling. Hazily, Aunty Ming was partly aware of people paying their respects to Uncle Ming and to her; and Ah Wai trying his best to lead them away to drinks and food so she wouldn't be disturbed. She stared with empty eyes at the altar. They had used one of his recent photos – the one taken on his sixty-first birthday. That was hardly more than a year ago! It was shortly after they received the letter from Ah Wai.

She remembered that day well.

'Come on, old partner, what did Ah Wai say? The baby must be due soon.' Aunty Ming pressed her husband eagerly, hardly waiting for him to finish the letter.

'Yes, the baby's due in a month's time. And… ' Uncle Ming glanced at his wife, then stared at the letter again.

'What is it? They're not expecting difficulties, are they?' Aunty Ming became anxious.

'No, no. Not the sort you imagine. Ah Wai wants you to go and help look after the baby for the first few weeks.'

'That's wonderful. We have always wanted to visit them and they've always said they were too busy, now is our chance.'

'You don't understand, old partner. Ah Wai only meant for you to go. He said he couldn't afford two tickets, what with the baby's expense and all.'

'Oh.' Aunty Ming felt really disappointed. She looked at her husband's sunken and worry-lined face and sensed the deep hurt in him.

Uncle Ming was a primary school teacher and she had to work part time as a cleaner to augment his meagre income. Their hope was pinned on Ah Wai, their only son. They skimped and saved to send him overseas for a better education, living for the day when he would return the conquering hero, taking care of them in their old age. But Ah Wai had plans of his own. He had stayed on in the UK, married an English wife and had only returned fleetingly to show off his new bride. Never once did he offer to have the old folks with him. They had accepted this quietly, not even discussing much about it between themselves, for fear of causing greater heartache to each other. But they were hurt and bewildered by Ah Wai's behaviour. Maybe it was their own fault for sending him to the West. They were warned that the young in those countries do not respect, let alone take care of the aged! Still, they thought their Ah Wai would be different.

That day they had various conversations on Ah Wai's letter. Aunty Ming felt apprehensive about going to England alone. They had been married for more than forty years and had never been apart for more than a day. To be thousands of miles away and leave old partner on his own? Why, she couldn't do that. What could Ah Wai be thinking of?

'You will just have to tell that son of ours I can't leave you alone here without anyone to look after you.'

'Now don't be hasty, old partner. Let's mull over this a little.' Uncle Ming said in that gentle, patient manner of his.

Three weeks later, she was in Manchester, 8,000 miles away from home. Uncle Ming had finally convinced her he was quite capable of taking care of himself for a couple of weeks. Ah Wai's house was in a very leafy part of town – she later found out it was one of the richest areas in Manchester. It stood in its own ground with a huge garden; and the number of rooms! There were five bedrooms, and two of them even came with bathrooms and toilets! Back home, five families with children would have lived comfortably within its walls. Ah Wai and his wife Angela owned a car each. Aunty Ming looked at all the luxuries around her and couldn't help wondering how could it be that Ah Wai couldn't afford another ticket for his father.

•

'Jimmy, can you tell your mum she must check the temperature of the formula using a clean thermometer, like the way I showed her, and not her fingers, please?' Angela frowned impatiently at her husband. She was certain her mother-in-law did it just to annoy her. 'And while you're at it, can you tell her to cook less of those funny soups? My curtains're beginning to smell like a Chinese restaurant.'

Jimmy! So what's wrong with the name Ah Wai? Couldn't the English master a simple name like that? Aunty Ming heard her querulous tone and guessed that Angela must be complaining against her again. These white-skin women all think they know so much. Running around barely two weeks after birth. Whoever heard of this! Wait till she's sixty years old – all her joints will scream with rheumatism and she'd remember her mother-in-law's advice then! She felt peeved when she thought of the hours she spent cooking the recuperative soup for the daughter-in-law when she was still in hospital only to discover Angela never actually touched a drop of it. All her effort was poured down the drain!

'Full moon' for baby Roger came and went. To Aunty Ming's dismay there was no proper observation of traditional ritual at all: the baby's head wasn't shaved like it should have been, there was no distribution of red eggs and vinegared ginger; and all that blue colour! Ah Wai should know only red should be worn to ensure good luck would always follow the young child. Her altercation with Ah Wai was to no avail.

'Look Ma, we did have a barbecue here when Angela came back from the hospital with Roger, remember? Anyway, Angela and I are not interested in superstitions like these, and who wants to eat cold red-dyed eggs and funny tasting ginger anyway.'

Aunty Ming looked resignedly at her son. All western clothes on the outside and western ideas in his head. With his skin pale from living so long in this country, he could almost pass for a white if not for his eyes and black hair.

•

Sundays had become her favourite day in this uncomfortable, strange land; because Sundays meant a possible visit to Chinatown, though, more often than not, Ah Wai would disappoint her, being too busy with his own engagements. Standing in the midst of Chinatown square, she gazed lovingly at all the Chinese faces around her, luxuriating in the chatter of familiar dialects in her ears. Isolated in Ah Wai's suburban home, Aunty Ming felt as if some of her senses had been taken away: everything was in English, even Ah Wai's Cantonese sounded oddly Anglo-Saxon through lack of usage.

'Aunty Ming. Have you eaten your fill?'

It was Grandma Luk, calling out the customary greeting to her.

'Grandma Luk. Yes, I have. And you?'

'I have had my fill. Ah Wai doesn't bring you down often, does he? I wish you could join our Mah Jong sessions.'

'So do I, if only to hear another Chinese voice. Ah Wai is very busy and I'm too scared to take the train by myself. Anyway, the baby's quite a handful so I doubt I'd have time to join your games,' Aunty Ming answered, a touch of wistfulness in her voice.

'Are you more used to the cold now? You must take care to wear warm socks and woollen underwear. Us oldies not strong like the young ones, our joints are more fragile.'

'I know. That's why I'm down today. I want to buy some herbs to make soup to warm up the blood. Everything's so expensive here though. I'm still not used to the prices – and the quality's not half as good.'

'Oh you'll get used to it. We all have to make do. Where is the rest of the family? How are you getting along with your daughter-in-law? Must be difficult when you're not able to talk the same language.'

'Oh, it's not too bad. Ah Wai interprets for us, and anyway, with them both working now I hardly get to see them.' Aunty Ming did not wish to complain about Angela, or her son, for that matter. It was not good face to admit she did not really enjoy the revered position of a mother-in-law. 'Here's Ah Wai. I must go. Talk to you next time I'm in town.' Aunty Ming bade farewell to her friend when she saw Ah Wai approaching with Angela and baby in tow.

•

She put on her reading glasses and started to go through the letter again – for the third time. Aunty Ming missed her lifetime partner terribly, worrying about his meals and whether he stayed out too late on his evening walks. He sounded cheerful in the letter. The question wasn't asked but she knew he would be wanting her return. With each passing month, Aunty Ming was getting impatient herself. First Ah Wai said after baby's full-moon, which was reasonable. Then Angela decided to return to work early and Ah Wai said could she stay for a couple more weeks till they established a reliable baby-sitter. The weeks had now turned into months. Aunty Ming was beginning to wonder if Ah Wai made any effort at all. Aunty Ming took off her glasses to wipe away the tears that had somehow started to flow. She must talk to Ah Wai again about returning.

'Ma, Ma! Can I come in?' Ah Wai pushed open the door without waiting for her reply. He looked dazed. She noticed a hint of tears in his eyes.

'What is it Ah Wai? Something happened to your Pa, isn't it?' A strong sense of foreboding rose up in her mind. Aunty Ming silently prayed she was wrong.

'Yes ma, I'm afraid it's bad news, they found Pa by the river, he's... Ma!'

Aunty Ming had collapsed before Ah Wai could finished his news.

The next day Ah Wai organized for the two of them to go back immediately. As the baby was too young to travel, Angela had stayed behind. Aunty Ming was beyond consolation. She listened numbly as Ah Wai told her how their neighbour Mui Yee had found Uncle Ming lying faced down by the river, under a willow tree, late in the evening. Mui Yee had been entrusted to take care of Uncle Ming's meals in her absence. Alarmed by his failure to turn up long after dinner time, Mui Yee had gone out searching for him. Uncle Ming died before arrival of the ambulance. There was nothing anybody could do. The doctor had diagnosed a heart attack. Aunty Ming knew why he was out there on that evening – it was their forty-second anniversary and he must have gone to their favourite spot by the river to commemorate it.

•

'Ma, I have to go back to work soon. Are you sure you won't come with me? Now that Pa's dead, why don't you come and stay with us?' For the umpteenth time since the funeral, Ah

Wai was trying to persuade his mother.

Aunty Ming only shook her head. She had abandoned her old partner late in his life. She would not leave him again. Feelings of grief and guilt totally consumed her. She had no idea how she would carry on alone without her old partner. One thing was certain though: she was through playing nanny and maid for the son.

The Diary of Walter Chan

K. P. William Cheng

8 March

I'm gay, and I'm Chinese. I knew I was gay when I was ten. I knew it when I became British. But Angel doesn't understand. She doesn't understand a thing. This is why we had a massive argument this afternoon.

We met up for lunch at the Mandarin Hotel. It was round about half twelve and we began talking as soon as we sat down. She asked me what had been happening since I got back from York. I did not know how to start, and I began telling her about Mum. It was a fact that Mum's character had changed quite a lot since father's death.

The conversation then turned to my sexuality. I still couldn't bring myself to tell her my real feelings. She had blamed me for not being strong enough in character. But did she realise that I had tried very hard to suppress my own feelings? She still could not accept my so-called different life-style. She was getting a bit impatient, and I tried my best to convince her that there was nothing wrong with me. She said that being a Chinese I had to marry a Chinese girl and settle down and have half a dozen children. She also said I was upsetting the traditional ideology. I did not argue with her – I could have. I did not want our relationship to deteriorate simply because my sexuality was different from what she wanted. Besides, I thought I was not doing anything wrong – I was not harming other people. I was not a thief, or a bank robber, and my life was as normal as anyone else's. Why couldn't she accept the truth? I told her that Arthur might be coming to see me during summer.

11 March

I rang William tonight because it is his twenty-second birthday. He was pleased to hear my voice, so he said, but maybe he was making impatient gestures while talking to me. I told him I could not afford to miss College another day. The Degree is eating me up. I also tried to tell William about my extraordinary meeting with my sister a few days before. He didn't sound very interested, I suppose he is far too busy with Robert Owen. Anyway he shouldn't complain. We talked at my expense and I'm just worried about the massive phone bill my mother is going to receive. I told William that I would be back in England a week later. He said he would pick me up in Manchester. How nice! He is always the sweetest friend in my life. I honestly don't know what I'd do without him pointing out all my faults, even though sometimes he can be very irritating.

I sometimes really wish I were William. At least he does not have any obligation to his family. And from what he told me it is very unlikely that he will return to Glasgow and his parents after the Degree. I envy his freedom. Why is he allowed to do whatever he wants while I'm stuck with a big problem?

I wish I had a joint tonight. I wish William was here and we could get stoned together like the old times and talk about anything and laugh at everything.

16 March

I was reading *Death of a Salesman* this afternoon when all of a sudden Mum woke up. She was calling my name in her bedroom. She might have been dreaming, but I'll never forget the frightened look on her face. She was sweating.

She asked me to go back to Hong Kong once I've finished the Degree so that she would have someone to stay in the house. She said that she would be lonely if I settled down in London. I could not bear to see her wretchedness – she was weeping – so I told her that I would fly back to H.K. as soon as my exams were finished. She felt a lot better when she had my reassurance, but when we had dinner, she brought up the subject again and said she would be happy if I lived with her after the Degree and she was thinking of giving up the flat in London. I told her not to worry too much, and then we ate in silence. I reckon I will have to give up my dream of settling down in England and having a quiet and enjoyable life. I can't be selfish. I have to shoulder the responsibility. No matter how much I hate my birth place, no matter how much I want to settle down in London, I really have to think of the others.

18 March

Sitting in flight BA 028 I feel as if I'm abandoning part of my family. (Angel still gives me disapproving looks – I suppose there is nothing I can do to change what she now thinks of me.) I tried to be cheerful but father's death overwhelmed all the members of the family. The funeral was impressive. Money is all that matters in Hong Kong. I don't want to be rich. I don't want to be tied down by an endless mortgage. I don't want to live in a horrible place like Hong Kong. But what can I do? I feel I'm trapped. I live a totally different life from the rest of the people in Hong Kong. I simply have a different notion of life. After all I am not greedy. I do not hope to be extremely rich. All I am asking for is a comfortable, enjoyable and simple life. But I can't have this.

The flight is fairly empty. I am occupying three seats myself, putting my books on the seat next to me and my jacket and bag another seat. How can BA make a profit? No wonder the air tickets are so expensive. They have to keep the price as high as possible in order to cut down the loss. For some mysterious reason the air steward keeps staring at me every time he walks past my seat. Maybe he is interested in what I'm writing in this journal. Why are people so nosey? Actually he is quite attractive. I noticed him when I boarded the flight. I must say I like his soft blond hair most although he is very muscular. Maybe he's staring at me because I wear a red ribbon.

Just finished breakfast. It looked awful and it tasted awful. The only thing I ate was cheese on crackers, and I drank the orange juice. Still the air steward smiles whenever he walks past me. He must be gay. I can tell by his eyes. I'm not in the mood to cruise – I can't be bothered. Now he is fixing his eyes on my *The Works Of Alfred Tennyson.* What on earth does he want? The flight is supposed to land in about twenty minutes. I am anxious and I can't describe my feelings. I really look forward to seeing sweet William again. I also look forward to putting my foot on English ground. I miss England. William must have a lot of gossip for me.

19th March

I am literally exhausted. I can't write anything. I keep hearing annoying noises in my ears because of the turbulence of the flight. I was catching up with the latest gossip from William on the way back to York. We laughed nearly non-stop during the one and a half hour car journey. He bitched about Molly, Wiggy, Susan, Lizzy and last not least Fanny. He also told me that Paul was missing me because he bumped into him and Paul asked him where I was. It's nice to know that a straight guy like Paul does care about friends regardless of gender and sexuality. I wonder if he'd be surprised if I confessed my real feelings to him? Anyhow, it's just a fantasy!

Yes, the air steward is gay – it's confirmed. He was helping me to get my stuff (I'm not tall enough) from the overhead luggage space, and accidentally, or rather incidentally, his elbow hit my chest when he took the duty free bag out. He apologised and seizing the opportunity he asked me my name, and I told him. He said sarcastically to me that Walter didn't sound like Chinese, and I said to him 'Don't be so rude. A rose by any other name would smell as sweet.' He was quite astonished by my poetic power – thanks to Juliet Capulet.

Anyway we went through the usual stuff like where do you

come from, where do you live, what do you do, etcetera. So we swapped addresses, and he told me that he would visit me in York some time because he had never been to this 'historic city'. I thought you wouldn't like to stay in York because there is nothing there. I can't even wait to get out of this boring dump. Anyway his visit is something I can look forward to. He is quite nice after all. I wonder what Arthur would say if I told him I was chatted up by an air steward.

23 March

Essays, essays, and essays. More essays. My life is dominated by essays. I'm sick of bloody essays. I've two essays to be in by the end of the month. How am I supposed to cope with all these boring essays? The college is suffocating me. Talked to Arthur over the phone. He said it was cold in Stockholm – the only thing he can say to me these days. I told him what happened in Hong Kong and about my extraordinary encounter with the air steward. He is not a bit jealous. I wish he was. At least it shows he cares for me. I said I'd be back in Hong Kong this summer and asked him if he really wanted to meet me there. He said yes, thank God. I thought for one minute he did not want to see me anymore. This is why I hate long distance relationships – the person is simply not there when you most need him. I was crying hysterically when I got the news of father, and Arthur was not there to calm my anguish and sorrow.

20 April

Got a call from Edward, the gorgeous air steward I met last month. I was surprised. I thought he was kidding when he said he was coming to York, but obviously he meant it. He asked if it was convenient for him to stay for two nights at my place. I said it was fine, and told William I would have a guest this weekend. All he said was 'Is he good-looking?' What a tart. Then William asked me 'Are you in love?' Of course not.

How could I be in love with someone to whom I have only talked for about five minutes? The fact is that I can't even recollect the face of this air steward!

25 April
I think I'm getting too emotionally attached to Mr Air Steward. Over the past two nights I did not sleep well at all and my penis is well-abused. Sex was magical with Edward. Of course we did everything safe. I know what these air stewards are like. Edward seemed to know where my stimulation was – he must be very experienced. And I'm far too inexperienced. He brought me to a new horizon. Only now do I realise the miracle of sex. What does one expect when I've only been with just one guy all my life? Edward told me he would be in England again in about a fortnight. He asked me if I wanted to see him again. A subtle hint. I said I would like to meet him again. Unwittingly I fell in love with him after this two-night stand. More unwittingly I also told him about my Swedish boy-friend. He doesn't seem to be bothered, so what's that supposed to mean? Am I too naive in the world of homosexual relationships? The main thing is that I can talk a great deal with Edward and, amazingly enough, we share a lot of interests. We both like literature. We both like cinema and theatre. We both like classical music. More importantly we both like red wine, and drink a lot of it. In many ways we are compatible, and this includes sex. Oh Mr Air Steward is tormenting my mind!

1 May
Arthur phoned me and said he has booked the flight ticket to Hong Kong, though he has to change at Copenhagen. I must say I'm delighted to hear this. I miss him terribly. At this very moment I don't know what to do with my life. Can a person be in love with two guys simultaneously? I ask this because one minute after Arthur called, the phone rang again and I

was talking to Edward. I feel like a slut. And William said I am a slut. What am I going to do with my life? Arthur? Edward? Mum? Family? Hong Kong? London?

5 May
Spent a wonderful night with Edward. We went to see a local production of *Persuasion.* I sympathise immensely with Anne Elliot. I feel I am like Anne Elliot to a certain degree, but unlike her in many respects. Edward enjoyed the play a great deal. He even said that he would not mind seeing it again tomorrow night. I hear him coming out of the bathroom. I must stop writing.

8 May
I begin to like Edward more than I can imagine. He's definitely not a substitute for Arthur. Certainly not one of these rebound things as William suggested. I love him equally and as much as I do Arthur. Over the past three days and nights, I was blissful, even though I had to re-read both *The Princess* and *The Yellow Wallpaper* for examinations. The real problem now is that Edward will apparently be in Hong Kong in the middle of July, and he said he wanted to spend some time with me. I can't promise because Arthur will be there as well. Also Edward said he wanted to settle down in London and asked me if I wanted to live with him after the Degree. I was speechless when he suggested a relationship. What am I going to do with my life? My life is a mess.

14 June
All the bloody exams finished. Great! The whole Degree finished. Great! No more essays. Great! I start drinking after the exam, one bottle after another, and I'm in a constant state of tipsiness – even now. Tell everyone that I'm going back to Hong Kong next week. I've got to. All my friends try to persuade me to stay, saying 'Oh, Walter, why don't you come

down to London with me?' I say I can't. William is weeping. I don't want to leave him either. He's such a gorgeous guy. I'm going to miss your sweet balls. But I've promised Mum to go back and stay with her. Besides, she has sold the flat in London, so I would have nowhere to stay. I sometimes hate myself for being Chinese. And sometimes I hate myself for being too British. Can anyone tell me who I am?

3 July
It seems to me that my life is dominated by these words: obligation, consideration, responsibility, thoughtfulness and duty.

Working in Hong Kong is a nightmare, though I must admit I love being with Mum again after so many years of constant separation. I can't cope with the hypocrisy of the business world. I sometimes wonder and ask myself: Walter Chan, what the hell are you doing in Hong Kong? This is not the place for you. I hate the Hong Kong business world. I hate to communicate to people in English when you know very well that they can speak Cantonese, especially when their English is so bad. There is no way I can communicate with efficiency. This silly cow I was talking to today doesn't even know what 'dehydrated' means, and I had to say I was thirsty. Her knowledge of the English language was appalling, yet she wanted to show off. I could not stand her. It is a commercial world. Money is not the most important thing yet without it it is impossible to survive. I wish I were living in London. At least the air is cleaner.

6 July
Arthur is in the shower at the moment. Mum seems to like him although they have difficulty communicating with each other. Under my influence, Arthur has learnt some useful Chinese phrases – well, enough to talk to Mum I suppose. And Mum's English is just adequate to converse with Arthur.

What Angel will say when she meets Arthur is what I'm now worrying about. She is supposed to come back home this Saturday, and I do believe that she will criticise anything Arthur does and says, trying to put me off him or trying to put him off me. I believe she is determined to split us up.

I must say I feel good tonight, since Arthur is here with me after such a long separation. He kissed me on the lips when I met him at the airport. Fancy two guys showing intimate affections in the middle of Hong Kong Airport! I cannot even imagine this in the city centre of London. I felt a lot of people at the airport were staring at us. But I don't care. As long as I'm with Arthur I feel happy. I have taken a day off work tomorrow so I can show Arthur around the scenic spots of Hong Kong – there aren't many though, not as many as London anyway. I hope he enjoys his stay here. Apparently he's going to stay with me until he feels like going back to Stockholm. Now what am I going to do with Edward? He is supposed to be calling me next week. I'm trapped in a moral dilemma.

7 July

Had an extremely wonderful day with Arthur – this is the miracle of love. We went everywhere, and everywhere was hustle and bustle. I guess Arthur was a bit overwhelmed today. It's a shame that we forgot to bring the camera with us, otherwise we could have pretended we were the silly tourists running around in the streets of Hong Kong.

While we were having a glitzy meal at the Holiday Inn Hotel, Arthur told me how much he had missed me over the past few months. He was at one point hinting that he would not mind settling in Hong Kong with me. I honestly said to him that I did not want to stay in Hong Kong. But he was right to point out the fact that I have to look after my mother from now on. I did not keep the secret about Edward either. Arthur was very understanding but said he wanted me to stop seeing Edward. I did not know what to say. I felt like I was cheating him.

So when he took a rest on the bed reading a Swedish book I stole the opportunity to ring sweet William. He is having a good time in London and has a fascinating job with Marks and Spencer. I told him my situation and he said that I should stick to Arthur because Edward is not offering any stability to me. True. Besides I know Arthur more and Edward is like an infatuation, maybe a rebound, so it's better to forget Mr Air Steward. He said we all make mistakes, but we must learn from mistakes. What's that supposed to mean? I also told William how much I wanted to go back to England. But he doesn't want to interfere with my life. Right now I just need a bit of encouragement and I'll book myself a flight ticket back to London. Anyway it's a dream. William said he would be going to Gran Canaria with Rodney in August. Typical. That means I would not see him again until the Degree ceremony in September.

8 July

Angel was kind to Arthur! I reckon it's mainly because Arthur turns out to be someone who is the total opposite of what she expected. She expected a thin, ugly, effeminate and shrill drama queen. But when she saw Arthur was a six-foot two, muscular, young, handsome and straight-acting guy, she was ever so nice to him. Apparently they like each other, and I am slightly jealous even that Arthur has pinched all Angel's attention today. I am also annoyed that at one point they made fun of some of my personal secrets. Now Arthur has obtained more inside information on me and yet I still have not talked to his brother in Gothenburg. It's not fair. I was talking to Axel while Mum was busy cooking. He seems to like Arthur too. I heard them talking briefly in German, but as usual he keeps quiet most of the time. So I asked Axel if he could place Arthur anywhere in his company, and he said it was no problem.

Arthur is pleased. It means he will be living in Hong Kong with me and Mum. Angel is delighted to hear this – actually it was she who suggested to her husband that Arthur could work for Public Relations, since he can speak several languages. Once again Axel is induced by his manipulative wife!

10 July

Arthur says to me that he is happy to live with me and Mum. Thank God! All the problems solved! I was quite worried that he would want to rent an apartment with me near the city centre, and I did not want to leave Mum alone. Actually, Mum is getting better every day. I think she is used to her life now. Every now and then she mentions father, but she is able to control her emotions and try to laugh things off. Arthur likes Mum immensely for some reason. Maybe it's because she cooks everything he likes for him, and as long as he has delicious food he is friendly to anyone despite the language barrier. Besides, Mum has taught him a few more Chinese phrases, and I was quite surprised tonight that Arthur told me not to disturb him in Chinese whilst he was watching television. Mum is certainly corrupting my husband.

11 July

Why? Why? Why? Edward wants to meet up for a drink and a meal tomorrow, and I said yes without consulting Arthur. I am so selfish. Arthur doesn't seem to mind, he sounded as cold as possible. But I know that deep inside he is jealous. I reassure him that it would be nothing more than a drink and a meal, and I promise that I will tell him I am going to settle down with him (Arthur) in Hong Kong no matter how much I hate the city. It's going to be one of these horrible days for me tomorrow. Arthur ignored me when I said 'I love you sweet babe' before he left the bedroom for a shower.

6 September

The Degree Ceremony went well and it was so nice to see William again this morning. For the first time in my life I loved the air of York! But I love London better. High up in one of the rooms at the Hilton Hotel, Arthur and I can oversee the glitzy Hyde Park. A real park. So green. So tranquil.

Selected Extracts From The Personal Journal Of A British Born Chinese

Florence Li

March 10th

Melissa has just rung me in a flood of tears. We spent two and a half hours on the phone. Her dad is presently having a cow because he's found out that she's going out with Matthew (the English guy that lives down the road from her). Still, it has taken him six months to find out about them, so at least she was happy for six months. She told me that she was thinking of leaving home. I asked her to think about it seriously. I mean, it's no place for any lone Chinese girl out there. The number of times that I've covered for her while she was seeing Matt is uncountable. I don't mind though, because they make a great couple.

… Mel said that her dad went absolutely beserk and started ranting and raving about how she'd successfully brought down the family name and how they'd now be a huge laughing stock. Mel said he kept repeating 'We've got no face! We've got no face!' I think that he's mistaken the 'We' for 'I'. He's only concerned about saving his own ugly face. He's threatened to go out and kill the 'Gwai Jy' for 'stealing' his daughter, but Mel's older brother calmed him down. What annoys me the most about her dad is that when Mel's brother was seventeen he had an English girlfriend, but when his dad found out there wasn't any fireworks – not even a spark. Sexist or what?

March 12th

I hate to say this, but Mel's dad was right. On Sunday I was in Chinatown with Mum when she got called over to a group of her friends. Those friends have tongues on them so sharp that they have to be careful they don't cut themselves – they're all granny perms with big mouths and designer handbags.

Anyway, one of her fogey friends asked her whether she knew anything about 'Mel and her Gwai Jy boyfriend'. They wanted to know things like whether she had slept with him or not. I don't understand why they would even want to know about things like that. I mean, me and Mel don't sit there wondering about a particular fogey and her bedroom antics – errgg, the thought is just too disgusting! Although Mum had knowledge of stuff, she was dragged off by yours truly in a desperate attempt for the WC. Mum was absolutely dying to dish the dirt – and it showed. If Mel's boyfriend had been black their tongues would have been working overtime.

March 17th

Jason's mum and dad deliberately came round today to show me up. 'Jason's going to Cambridge Uni!' His mother practically sung it into my forced smiley face. Apparently he got a place there because he's a clever little blighter. God, have they honestly got nothing better to do than gloat? Somehow, no. Admittedly Middlesex Poly doesn't possess the same RINGG to it like Cambridge – and by God, didn't Jason's oldies know it!

April 19th

Matt introduced Mel to his parents and they were really nice to her, not at all racist. They even invited her to tea. Matt was really distressed the couple of weeks before, when Mel wasn't allowed to see him – following her dad's strict inhumane orders, Mel had to go to college and come home straight away. It was only recently that she began telling her dad that she had to do netball practice, so she could see Matt for at least an hour. She prefers to stay at his house where it's 'safer'.

April 21st

Apparently Mel's brother was driving past while she was on her way to Matt's. He told her dad, who confronted her. Mel just stopped what she was doing and ran out, where she called me from a phone box to pick her up.

I drove her back to my house, but Mum was against her staying. It 'wasn't the proper Chinese thing to do'. Stuff Chinese morality and all that. I eventually convinced Mum to let her stay the night, but only if she called her folks to tell them she was alright.

Mel tried to call home five times that night and each time there was no answer, which was strange because normally they would have been working.

Mel decided never to speak to her brother ever again, not after he grassed her up. If Mel's dad had been more easy-going then Mel wouldn't even have to sneak behind his back in the first place. Mel feels so trapped. Her dad was yelling at her that she would have no concentration for studying if she continued to see the 'Gwai Jy', but no matter what, Mel couldn't communicate with her dad. It wasn't just the fact that there was a language barrier there, but also because she felt that it would be pointless to even try to talk to her dad, he just doesn't understand. Her dad thought that she was just like all the other teenage girls that he saw when he was working in the shop on a Friday night, the ones that are totally pissed out of their heads, the ones who are basically thick as pig shit, the ones that end up being mothers by the time they're sixteen. Mel isn't stupid. In fact, she's quite clever, despite what her father thinks of her.

April 22nd

Drove Mel back to her house at 1 pm. Her dad's car wasn't there. I walked upstairs with her to her lounge and found her mum there, her face cut and bruised. She was a total wreck.

May 10th

Mel has finished with Matt. Although she still likes him loads, she can't bear to see her mum in a state. She hopes it's for the best.

June 19th

Mum dragged me down to Chinatown today. I really despise going now, for fear of bumping into one fogey after a-sodding-nother. Not exactly my ideal day. I now have full second hand knowledge of the time, date and venue of where Mrs. Chan's Henna will take place and also which flight Cheung will be taking out to the Bahamas later this week, on Wednesday to be correct. Yawn, yawn, yawn.

July 30th

Mel's gone. I'm sad that my best friend has now gone, but she and her mum really did need to get away from her bastard father. Even my mum and dad admit it.

Mel rung me from the train station bound for Birmingham, where she'll be staying with her auntie for a while.

Today I got an offer from Middlesex Poly which I'm thrilled about, because it means that I won't have to see the fogies for a while!

You Never Know Who You Might Bump Into

Florence Li

Joanna had a maths assignment to finish and her cousin Christy was round to help her. They had been at it for just ten minutes when Joanna had an inkling that Christy was about to ask something. She was constantly looking at her – as if to find the right moment. Sure enough, the moment came. But nothing prepared Joanna for what Christy said next.

'Come on then what is it?'

'Someone's asked me to ask you something.'

Joanna groaned. Christy always used that phrase when she was about to set her up with a date. The problem was, although they liked the same types of food and shared the same tastes in clothes, when it came to men, Christy and Joanna's ideas were as different as Bacardi and Coke.

'Peter's asked me to ask you if you'd, well, like to go out with him.'

Jo's pen dropped to the table, her face screwing up like she had just swallowed one of her gran's miracle herbal remedies. 'No way! Absolutely no way! Are you totally out of your mind?'

'Oh go on Jo, Pete's a really nice guy, he's in his second year at UMIST reading engineering, his dad owns a restaurant in Chinatown, he drives a brand new Toyota Celica and, he's quite cute… ' Chris reeled it off so magnificently it was almost as though she had been practising.

'No.'

'Oh, please will you go out with him? Look, if you don't like him after one date then you never have to see him again. Go on, what do you say? For your cuz, eh?' said Christy.

Joanna knew why Christy was so obsessed with Chinese

men. Every night, after college, Christy would place herself in front of the television and video, ready for the night's installment of the latest TVB musical spectacular or, equally as good, the latest situation comedy starring the current Chinese fit bit/flavour of the month. Her bedroom was covered wall to wall with the Andy Laus, Aaron Kwoks and David Leung type of guys. All the men on Christy's wall shared one common feature apart from being Chinese and famous: these guys were the types that parents would kill for – they were squeaky clean, with shining haloes and brilliant toothy smiles.

But they were too sickly for Joanna to bear. They were boring and lifeless.

She could only describe Chinese men as belonging to one of two camps, both deemed highly unsuitable (not to mention a health risk) for any hip British Chinese chick living in the Nineties. In the first camp, Jo placed the Chinese father, the usually short, dumpy, quiet, boring object that cohabited with the rest of the family. In Joanna's mind every Chinese family possessed one, except her friend Carrie's. Hers had a receding hairline.

The other type of Chinese guy was the frail, sheepish looking chippy worker, looking forever in his pre-pubescent years, despite usually being in his twenties. Chesney Chan was such a guy and, apart from being the honoured recipient of the most ridiculous name award, was, unfortunately for Joanna, related through her mum's tragic and sad side of the family.

Now the Gwai Jys at her school were something else. Unlike Chinese guys, Gwai Jys seemed to understand the concept of fun, and didn't long for any long term commitment. You read in Chinese newspapers every day of how the current-day Romeo leapt off a tall building to his death, all because the Juliet became a bit bored by the commitment. It might seem far fetched, but seriously, Chinese guys did have a tendency to get too serious too soon and this put Joanna off.

'So, where am I going with Peter, then?' Joanna asked her cousin about the big date, in a ho-hum sort of manner.

'What! Are you saying that you'll go out with him, then?' Christy's mouth turned up at the points.

'Yes, but only this once. Only one date, okay?' Joanna said, beginning to regret having said yes. 'So, when is it?' Joanna asked her again.

Christy had a massive, Cheshire cat-like smile on her face. 'Oh, tonight…'

'Tonight? Tonight?!! You could have given me a bit more notice!!'

'Calm down, will you… I don't know why you're fretting so much. After all, you normally don't even give Chinese guys a second look. For Pete's sake! Whoops, sorry!'

Unlike her scruffy cousin, Joanna liked to look her best wherever she went, even if it was just to the local post box directly opposite her house. 'You never know who you might bump into' was her motto. She took a couple of forced, deep breaths. 'Okay, so tell me *where* am I going to meet him, *what time* and *what* I'm going to be doing…' Joanna needed to know – it was absolutely a matter of life or death.

'I'm not sure…' Chris broke off. She handed her a piece of paper. 'But he did give me this, and he wants you to ring him if you're going and if you're not, then don't bother.'

Joanna read the number. It began 0850. 'Oh great, a bleeding mobile phone number,' she thought.

Christy pushed the phone towards Joanna.

'Oh well, here goes. All or nothing!' Jo took one last sigh and pressed the digits carefully but quickly. The phone began to ring. She cleared her throat several times before she was interrupted by a deep male voice.

'Hello?'

'Oh, hello, erm… my name's Joanna Yau… I…'

'Oh, hello! I was waiting for you to ring and I'm glad you did!' Already Peter's voice sounded welcoming. 'So you got

45

my message, then? Can I take this as a 'Yes'?'

'You're pretty confident of yourself, aren't you?' Joanna was intrigued. It was unlike any Chinese guy to be so confident – it was unusual, unique and Joanna liked it.

Listening in, Christy could tell things were going okay from the way Joanna's voice seemed less tense – she was even laughing at one point.

'Okay, I'll see you tonight at nine then, bye!'

Christy interrupted Joanna's daydream: 'So, what do you think, then?'

Joanna landed back on earth with a thump.

'Is he nice, then?' Chris continued.

'Mmm… ' Her daydream was cut off when it suddenly dawned on her. 'Oh my God! I've got nothing to wear – help me, Chris!!!'

Violin Practice

Hi Ching

It was boring, boring, boring. He was already fifteen, which he had reached six months ago. Surely that was old enough to have some kind of independence? English boys didn't have to suffer such restraints! Every night the chains came out and the drawbridge was brought up! Why did they continue to treat him like the contents of a can of beans! Didn't his parents realise it was almost the 21st Century, London? Not ancient China?

'You can't go. Who is this Janet Jackson? Michael Jackson's sister? Publicity hungry weirdos. Do you want to end up like him? Crazy!'

Huang's father was reading a report and his mother was dishing out white boiled rice onto dinner plates.

'Too much!' yelled his younger brother Lo.

'It's not much. You need to eat,' mother said firmly.

'I'm not hungry!'

'Why not? Why don't you eat? You are too thin. Don't you like my food?'

'I hate rice.'

'You've always eaten rice.'

Father piped in, 'you should be pleased your mother takes the trouble to cook you such good food. Other people only get TV dinners.'

Huang thought of his friends. Allowed to make arrangements to meet at Bank. Allowed to catch the Docklands Light Rail to the London Arena. Allowed to go to see Janet Jackson in concert. Whereas he, a full fifteen and a half, was constantly forbidden to go out to see 'that rubbish'.

Father was always so serious. He hardly ever laughed. If he did, it just came out like a smirk.

'Now, if it had been Joshua Bell. That would have been a different matter. That boy's violin playing is an inspiration. Something for you to aspire to. There's no talent in jumping up and down like a lunatic. Anyone can do that!'

Of course anyone could do that. Question was, whether one was allowed!

'Aren't you eating?' his mother said.

She could see he wasn't eating. That he was sulking. That his appetite had gone. That was the annoying thing about her. She couldn't say 'You are not eating.' She had to skirt round the issue and say 'Aren't you eating?' when it was abundantly clear to anyone he wasn't eating.

'I really don't know what is wrong with you two boys. You just don't appreciate your parents. Look how your mother works all day in the kitchen just preparing tasty food for you to eat. Hamburgers. That's all you ever want. And chips. Eat up!'

Commands here. Commands there. Do this. Do that. Appreciate this. Appreciate that. Be grateful for this. Be grateful for that.

'Stop sulking.'

'I'm not sulking.'

'Then get rid of that unpleasant scowl on your face. And eat your dinner.'

Huang attempted to shovel food into his mouth and chew. If only his father could see how unpleasant he himself looked. And he couldn't understand why his mother put up with all this crap. Modern women aren't meant to be subservient, tiptoeing round their husband's every need. Why didn't she have a job? Get some self-respect instead of staying home to cook and clean for the family. There were lots of things he couldn't understand.

'Don't be unhappy, Huang,' his mother said. 'Pa knows what's best for you. When you mature, you'll understand.'

What did she mean understand. Had she read his mind?

His face must have revealed something. Maybe he should watch his expressions. Or not? Maybe he shouldn't hide anything. Well, not his thoughts anyway. But it was difficult to say anything without getting his head bitten off. What was wrong about going to a pop concert! Was to experience Janet Jackson 'live' a bash at morality? She was definitely what Huang would call liberated. And sexy too. Yeah. Sexy. With her voluptuous boobs and curvy hips. Something one could grasp! Sweat! One could feel her heartbeat racing. Not like those etiolated, finely spun, every hair in place Chinese songstresses with the total good taste look. You could bet your bottom pound they never sweated! They probably didn't even have pores. Just stretched skins of scrubbed latex and fibreglass expressions.

Oh hell! He just noticed. He was eating awful scented pork with five spice powder fried with bean sprouts and mange tout and baby corn and other indefinable things. Why do the Chinese always season their food to indistinction! What's wrong with a plain fresh salad of simple fresh vegetables? Just why does everything have to be so chopped up all the time, mangled and marinated in a ton of spices, and fried in litres of oil and cornflour? Oleaginous. That best described it. He liked that word. He just looked it up the other day. Oleaginous food! Chomp, chomp, chomp. He could feel the food rotating round and round his mouth. Good thing everything was cut up. If it had been a piece of steak, he would have lost the battle to chew long ago.

Lo was also toying with his food. They exchanged glances of disgust.

'Is there something bothering the two of you?'

There she goes again. Wasn't it clear to her they hated her food?

'Try some of this liver.'

Liver. Yuck. Fried pig's liver. Bloody fried pig's liver.

'So tender.'

49

And so sickening. As you bit into it, you could feel the blood squirt into your mouth's interior. Like Reservoir Dogs. Or so Huang had heard. He'd never seen it. It had just come out on video and he looked too young to sneak into the cinema like some of his other friends. In fact, he had a hard time persuading people he was fifteen.

Lo was choking. 'I don't like liver. I hate the taste.'

'Try to get used to it,' his mother said.

'Why do I have to eat it?'

'It is very nutritious.'

'I don't care.' Lo spat out the liver.

'Why did you do that?' his father asked.

'I don't like it!'

'Do you know how many people are starving around the world. Have you never seen on the TV? All those people in Ethiopia? Did you see how skinny they are? Never waste food.'

The parents rounded on their son. The old stories about grandfather and grandmother hungry during the war were aired all over again. The same old parables about Chinese refugees fleeing from the mainland. The boat people, all hungry. Starving. Dying on board ships. Drowning.

Huang wished he could stick out his hand and squeeze and yank his father's balls really really hard so that they could be flung into a pot of soup to boil like all those floaty sacs of wan ton. That would shut him up good and proper! Trouble was, he could never see them. Not even when father was in swimming trunks. Huang always thought about the family's male privates. He even measured his own with a ruler. Barely four and a half inches even when erect! Whereas Mick at school had one six inches long, relaxed! How was that possible?

'Your room is looking a little messy, Huang. Better try and tidy it up before the maid comes tomorrow to clean.' His mother leaned over to put another dollop of fried liver on his plate. Always cleaning for the maid, Huang thought.

His mother was wearing a white blouse buttoned up to her

neck as usual. You could never see her breasts. They were always clamped under hordes of buttons. They must be tiny and flat. If only she would release her hair that was always tied up in a bun. Be spontaneous for once. Let the hair fall in luscious curls round her neck. And when she leaned over, may she have voluptuous breasts that would fall smack into his face where he could bury his head possessively. Into her exposed cleavage.

These thoughts made Huang feel guilty. Surely it was wrong for sons to have such shameful thoughts about their mothers? But they had been occurring for some time now. What brought them on? And whenever his mother wore slacks, he always looked at her crutch, aware of the slight and narrow slit between her legs. He couldn't help it. These thoughts just occurred. If only he were a Catholic. Then he could go and confess. Chinese had no religious tradition of confession. Meditation was all very well but there was nobody you could unload your sins to. It was always codes of morality, analects, filial behaviour. One wasn't even allowed to sin!

Lo had thrown up again. Mother was cradling his face and pacifying him as father admonished. She was always touching Lo. Like she used to touch Huang until he became a man. Why wouldn't she touch him now? He wanted her to embrace him warmly and hold him tight like she used to when he dozed in front of the TV. These memories made him want to pick up a sword and shield and attack Lo. Like the Romans in their computer game. Swishing and swatting each other in their plumed helmets and metal breastplates. Instead, he held Lo's hand and stroked it.

For some obscure reason, Lo's hand felt greasy, like a condom. It was unbelievable. How did things get all tangled up like that? Ever since Huang discovered condoms and the pleasure one got jerking off in them, he stole moments whenever he could – sneaking in a few precious minutes before his showers, between lessons in the school loo, to give himself a vigorous rub. He could have as much fun without a condom, except the lubrication heightened his senses so much more. And then, after he had ejaculated, he always had a hard time trying to get rid of the slimy feeling of grease that clung on, smeared to his prick and hand.

Sexual images of people would flash through his mind. Shapes of legs and breasts, naked males, females, pulsing lips, hairless thighs. He must be going mad. He thought of these things all the time. Anything could trigger it off! He would get erections at the mere rhythm of a train, the vibration of a bus engine, the smoothness of the car seat, a glimpse of a woman's bottom tight in jeans...

'Hurry up and finish your meal, Huang! And stop fiddling with Lo's hand!' Another command from the head of the household. 'You should put in at least an hour's practice. When's your violin exam? Next week?'

The violin. Why the violin? Why not the guitar? What's so great about all this classical music. 'It's so good for you. Refined expressiveness. Subtlety. Depth.'

Was that stuffy or was that not stuffy? And wasn't it funny how his parents never thought of giving him classical Chinese music lessons. Strange! And what was so great about classical western music anyway? Huang liked soul!

'Chinese violin? Ee ee or or. Is that what you want? How can we find a teacher here to teach you? We are not in Taiwan now you know.' Another father axiom!

'Have your orange first,' his mother said. 'Otherwise you will get indigestion.'

A vision suddenly materialised in front of Huang. Mother, gloriously standing in her white Greek toga on the Parthenon, the wind blowing her gloriously flying ebony mane, the shape of her very physical body unfettered by tight skirts and dresses. Father captive in chains, in rags of slavery, being dragged up the wide stone steps by his prick and Lo rushing around, brandishing his sword, screaming and yelling ineffectually.

Huang's thoughts were racing.

Mother was screaming. He had never known her to scream. Not in that abandoned manner. She was screaming, 'all this time I followed you. I did what you had to do. Everything I didn't agree with, I didn't disagree. I swallowed my pride. I stifled my despair. I gave up teaching to be your wife. To bring up our family. To be Mrs Guo, wife of Mr Guo. Then you brought me here. To this wretchedly damp country with all these cold people who cannot speak Chinese! It shattered me. I wanted a divorce. I wanted to go back to Taiwan. I wanted to rescue my life. I yearned to see my friends again, my parents, my brothers, my sisters. Enjoy our noisy festivals. Not to be imprisoned in a house in a quiet residential suburb filled with quiet noiseless people. But I stayed here, by your side, so that we wouldn't lose face.'

'Father, what do you have to say in your defence?' Huang cried.

'I worked hard. Long hours at the bank making lots of money for your comfort. For our children's comfort. I didn't want to come to this cold country either, where no one speaks Chinese and people don't understand how energising noisy bustle is. I gave you a life of luxury. You did not have to go and work long hours like I have to, everyday. Slave to the dictates of Head Office, slave to the stock market, slave to the financial markets. So that we can afford a maid. But all I wanted to do was write poetry and send you love letters. But how can you understand the pressure my father put me through. His friends, our system, Confucius.'

'And mother, defend yourself,' Huang shouted playing his violin madly.

'Look at me. My face. I have lost all the malleability of my youth. I have become moulded into an existence between two narrowest points. Within me is a seething canyon of emotions and unfulfilled desires. I am tired of living this way. I want to follow my passions. I am sick and tired of subservience. I want my release. To be free of being your wife. To be footloose, mad and desirable!'

Huang watched in amazement as his mother jumped into a fountain full of water, emerging naked through the wet of her transparent toga. The she started to sing. He had never heard her sing before. And her song was raw. Loud. Powerful. His mother was singing a Janet Jackson song!

His father looked on in disbelief. He tried to cover her body with his. He tried to shout her down. Drown out the lewd lyrics she was so crazily uttering. But it was impossible.

Lo appeared with a rope to tie father. Together with Huang, they tied him to a tree. Father was weeping. He had lost control. His wife was raging mad and his sons had captured him and secured him to a tree. They were taunting him while his wife was flinging herself through wind and water liberating herself.

'Father, I hate you,' Huang was screaming. 'Why do you never play with me? Why are you always so cold? Don't you love me?'

His father looked at him in horror. Huang was clinging on to him, sobbing, kissing him.

'Get off and behave yourself! You are shameful !'

'Love me, father. Love me. Love me like Pete's father loves him. Love me like Mick's father loves him. At least smile. Is it so much to ask to be loved? I am your son after all.'

And Huang started to kiss his father like he was a lover. All over his face, his neck, his chest. And his father was in tears, weeping the loss of his fatherhood, the tragedy of love irretrievably lost.

'Huang,' his father said sharply. 'Don't waste your time daydreaming. Go and practice!'

Huang looked at his father. Then looked at his plate. There was only orange peel there. What happened to the Parthenon? The tree? The fountain? He looked at his mother as she calmly and methodically cleared away the dinner plates. Nothing had changed. Everything was just as it was before. Boring, boring, boring.

Huang went up to his room and took out his violin. It will have to be Grade five again! He failed it last year. Why do his parents insist he takes these exams? It was obvious he had no talent to be a violinist. What was the point? He tuned the instrument. Then took out his walkman and switched it on. There was a Janet Jackson tape in there. Sexy! If he couldn't go to the concert, he was bloody well going to listen to her singing. He could imagine her gyrating then. A few months ago, he suddenly discovered he could do this. Practice his violin whilst listening to his walkman. A bit like jogging. Automatic muscular responses. The violin screeched into tune. Good thing for winter! The windows were closed. His parents were watching TV and couldn't hear him much. No one would bother too much about the fistfuls of mistakes.

The Funeral

Deniell Rebecca J Lawrie

When he was nearly sixty-six, and I was six, my sister's godfather disappeared.

No-one was unduly concerned. He had taken to muttering at strangers and shining torches at night. People had begun to avoid him. A few months later my sister read a newspaper article headed: *Mysterious Dead Chinee.* The police had found a Chinese man with green, crisp pound notes pinned tightly to his long-johns from head to toe like tacky wallpaper. He had been staying in rundown accommodation. Police records noted his address as 'Nelson Street, Chinatown, Liverpool.' That man was of course my sister's godfather – my friend Mr Wong.

Mr Wong had been a seaman. I loved Mr Wong secretly, because he brought me lots of presents and laughter. He listened to me. He always seemed to wear a little smile. He had a permanent golden tan caused by those long hours working at sea under the severe sun. He was a thin and tall man, though everybody seemed tall to me then since I was only six years old. His clothing reminded me of a wrinkled, used tea bag. He hated ironing. But in death, Mr Wong was unusually neat and tidy.

The concept of death was alien to me. I did not understand it. I asked my brother for an explanation, just before we attended Mr Wong's funeral.

'I'll bleeden KILL YER if yer don't 'urry up!' was my brother's menacing reply.

Being Chinese, Mr Wong had an appropriate farewell. He was claimed in death, not through blood ties, but by the binding sense of clan spirit. His funeral was almost as elaborate as Mao Tse Tung's!

By day, the funeral parlour was used as a dining room, a gamblers' gathering site, and a social centre where retired seamen drank whisky and rice wine out of small glass tumblers.

But now, on the evening of Mr Wong's funeral, flowers were displayed in every vacant space. Thick joss-sticks and sickly-sweet smelling incense burned at a slow, deathly pace. Smoke seemed to fill every nook and cranny, drifting into our very souls.

I looked around. Empty sweet jars stood on numerous book shelves, half hidden behind a greasy white sheet. Others, on show, were filled with thousand year old duck eggs; preserved as a delicacy and kept for special occasions. Crimson red envelopes, with gold-leaf writing were placed in an old tattered bamboo basket. They contained money and prayers which were to be burnt, as sacrifices to their Gods Of Life.

We lined up, like a bus queue, awaiting our turn to pay our last respects. We were dressed traditionally in white. It was my turn to see Mr Wong. I leaned forward. He seemed to be asleep. My mother spoke sternly, 'Don't touch!'

Who can resist flouting the signs that read: 'WET PAINT. DO NOT TOUCH'?

What did a dead person feel like? I thought. Is he really dead? Would he jump up and say it was only a joke? Dressed in military style funeral uniform, I was masked behind mourning formality. My mother told me to say good-bye to Mr Wong. She also told me to behave myself, but my fingers twitched with involuntary curiosity and I struggled with my conscience. To obey, or not to obey?

Suddenly, my finger launched itself towards Mr Wong's face like a preprogrammed rocket towards the moon. 'Mr Wong, wake up!' I whispered. He was stiff as hard-board. Shock chilled my bones and I quivered. Did he move? Icy water flowed through my veins, through sinews, through pores, drenching all feeling, all thought. Sweat dampened my starched silk mandarin collar. My throat constricted.

He was cold, stone cold, jade cold. I froze as if his stillness was contagious. We were linked by more than touch. His death was somehow my death.

Through the candle-lit gloom I became aware of my relatives, staring in horror. Suddenly my mother slapped away my hand, and I breathed again.

'Bloody idiot!' muttered my father.

'Tut-tut. Stupid girl,' the priest hissed. His breath was insufferable and he spat when he spoke.

After a severe reprimand, my eyes sunk down heavily towards the ground in deep shame and guilt. I could not fully understand my unforgivable crime. The humiliation was overwhelming. Unable to face people, I headed for the sanctuary of the ladies' toilets to nurse my wounded spirit.

I locked the huge Victorian styled, mahogany door behind me. Burning incense, the smoke of mourning, drifted eerily and drearily into the dim, solemn, dank room. Shafts of daylight, muted by the grimy panes, fell upon the old-fashioned toilet. It looked like a throne in a play. A long, rusty, cast-iron chain hung from a China clay bowl. Fat flies buzzed to and fro. They seemed unaware of their dead relatives abandoned on the dusty window sill. Spiders' cobwebs furnished the stained glass windows, their builders waiting patiently for their prey. Large, jet black, shiny cockroaches hid in the corners.

Sitting on the toilet seat, like a queen on her throne, I said to myself, 'I wish I was dead too! Then they would be sorry, and it would serve them right!' I nurtured my wrath like brewing broth on a raging fire. Tears rolled down my face, like a water fountain. 'What's happened to Mr Wong?' I kept asking myself. My elders had treated me unfairly, critically, hatefully. In fact they were just plain mean! My only hope was that Mr Wong would stop being dead soon. He'd explain.

I never saw Mr Wong's face again.

I still possess a few of his presents, which reflect his

eccentric character: one bamboo back scratcher; one bone handled jungle knife, and one hard-back autobiography of Winston Churchill. All his gifts smell like moth balls.

The Right Pair

Daniel Wong

I had often wondered what the point of sex was. A lot of panting and biting, a moment of unselfconsciousness and pleasure, then the inevitable orgasm followed by polite stroking, and finally your partner's turn to come.

This new guy was no different. Chinese, yes – like myself. Taiwanese even. And in Birmingham! I had never had an Oriental in Birmingham. But the sex was boringly formula.

Maybe because I was not committed enough to it. Maybe because I did not love this man, this relative stranger who I had already cooked for and allowed to stay the night. Or maybe because I knew he would never love me right.

Yet he said he was happy! Do I have unrealistically high expectations? I was already planning how to extricate myself from this relationship.

I yawned, and he asked if I was sleepy.

'A little,' I said.

'I won't allow you to sleep tonight!' he grinned.

'Really?' I replied. Spare me.

•

A week later, I resolved to end things. His English was too limited, and I spoke no Mandarin. Besides, he had told me that after his studies in a year's time, he was off back to Taiwan. So what was the point?

I began by talking of my last relationship with Alex, how I'd been hurt and was keen not to make the same mistakes again. He said he appreciated my honesty. Tears came to his eyes. I told myself not to feel manipulated.

He encouraged me not to think too much.

I agreed, but said that was the way I was.

He said that in this life, there was too much suffering. Was it not enough that when we met, we felt happy? Certainly he was, and he sensed that I might be too.

Oh, the folly of projection! Or maybe there was some truth in that, but I was shielding myself from it? Self doubt can really fuck you up.

He asked if it was over. Coward that I was, I said I wasn't a hard person, I wanted the possibility of love, and agreed that he also risked getting hurt when he had to leave next year. He told me that he'd thought about asking me to wait for him during his one month holiday abroad this year. More emotional shackles.

I related the equivalent story of Alex and Jenny, how I wanted children and had sacrificed a wonderful opportunity with her because of misplaced loyalty, waiting for Alex.

Now, at last, he was beginning to understand me. He admitted that perhaps he'd been a little selfish, thinking I could 'help' him. God help us! I can barely help myself.

'If you find someone better,' he said, 'then you should go with that person. Yes, just go.'

Self-sacrificing to say the least. I felt infinitely better. Have my cake and eat it. Selfish bastard!

No. Perhaps in a time of exploration, this was the right way forward. Not too many responsibilities or expectations. I remember how another ex had said: 'It's like buying a new pair of trousers. You don't buy the first pair you try on.'

'The difference is,' I had replied, 'trousers don't have feelings.'

Game Boy

D. K. Y. Lee

The intense heat of the July afternoon filled the small room. Raymond was lying on his stomach, nestling in the chaos of his unmade bed. Sunlight, harsh and metallic, penetrated the thin half-drawn curtains. The walls of Raymond's room were sellotaped with posters of red Porsches and kung fu stars in attitudes of attack. A calendar advertising the 'Kowloon Harbour Take Away' dangled from the door of an open wardrobe, accompanied by Raymond's abandoned polyester blazer. Raymond was oblivious to his surroundings. Sounds of routine preparations for the evening's custom drifted through the half-open door, but the only sounds Raymond was aware of were those issuing from the credit card sized game machine held tightly in his hands.

Downstairs the scene was one of controlled chaotic activity. Mrs Chun stood at the stainless steel sink tossing a wide colander of beansprouts. The fatigue of the previous night's work had not left her pale, unmade face. Her tiny figure, lost in a pink nylon overall, swayed unsteadily. Wearily, she lifted the dripping container and placed it on the table next to the cooking range which dominated the whole side of the cramped, unventilated kitchen.

Tina stood at the kitchen table slicing onions, eyeing her mother surreptitiously, noting her tiredness. She rested the wooden-handled cleaver on the chopping board for a moment, brushing away a stray lock of hair with the back of her hand in case she smudged her carefully applied make-up.

'Do you think these will be enough for tonight, Mum?' It always struck her as strange that speaking in Cantonese gave any voice a raucous, uninhibited quality, collective testimony to which could be found in any of the restaurants in Soho on a Sunday afternoon.

'You'd better ask your father,' her mother replied softly without looking up.

Tina repeated the question and looked to her father for a reply. Mr Chun stood by the table in hunched concentration. The evening's work had not yet begun but beads of sweat were already appearing on his balding head. He had been standing immobile for several minutes now, absorbed in deciphering a heavily creased letter. Mrs Chun struggled past her husband with a container full of prepared rice. There was a pause. Then Tina repeated her question with impatience, irritated at her father's inactivity so close to opening time. Mr Chun snatched the heavy brown-rimmed glasses from his face and waved the letter at his daughter in frustration.

'Oh! I can't understand! It's from school and they write something about 'truancy'. What do they want?'

Wiping her hands on a faded tea towel, Tina took the letter. Her expression darkened as she scanned its contents. With unease, and frustration at her own insufficient knowledge of Cantonese, Tina explained in her heavy, South East London accent, 'They want you to go in and see them. Ray's been bunking off.'

'What mean 'bunking'?'

''Bunking'. You know, not going to school.'

'What mean 'tru-an-cy' then?'

'That's what it means! Ray has been staying away from school for no good reason. They say that there's been no explanation or any record that he's been sick, so they want you to go in and explain.'

Mr Chun exploded with fury. He motioned for Tina to call her brother downstairs. His gaze fixed angrily on the floor. The two women stood shocked at the ferocity of his action. Tina moved to the foot of the stairs, fearfully obedient. Uncertainty in her voice, she called:

'... Ray!'

There was no response so she tried again. Her eyes never left her father's face. It was frozen in anger.

'What?' came the annoyed reply, 'I'm in the middle of something.'

'You'd better come down. Dad wants you!'

•

Instead of coming down immediately, Raymond continued with the game. His thumbs feverishly worked the minute buttons on the machine. Tina called him again and, with his concentration disturbed, he sighed, tossed the game on the bed and lunged down the narrow, badly-lit stairway.

His sister's face gave him sufficient warning of the nature of the abrupt summons. Raymond paused at the foot of the stairs and took a deep breath.

Mr Chun was still staring fixedly at the floor as his son appeared in the doorway, the bamboo curtain rattling behind him.

'What have you been doing, eh? Why so long before you come down?'

'Homework.'

'What kind homework?'

'French.'

'Where were you yesterday, eh?'

'What d'you mean? I was at school of course.'

'The whole day?'

'Yeah…'

'What's this then, eh?' Mr Chun thrust the letter at his son with trembling hand. Raymond acknowledged its contents by hanging his head, resigning himself to what was still to come.

'Sui jai! Hei yau chee lei! At school, eh? Even now at the last minute you still can't tell the truth!' He slipped into Cantonese as he continued: 'Where were you yesterday and all the other days? Pretending to be at school all this time! Where were you really, eh?' He lunged forward and took his son by the ear. As Raymond crumpled with pain, Mrs Chun, her face concerned and anxious, stepped behind her husband taking him by the shoulder, only to be shaken away as he released his grip.

'Mr Lo's wife says she saw you Wednesday afternoon in the amusement arcade. I didn't believe her. Told her it couldn't possibly be you and that she should mind her own business! Told her my son is a good student, you good for nothing!'

With one swift movement. Mr Chun delivered a heavy slap to the side of his son's face. Mrs Chun cried out in surprise and locked her arms around her husband's body to restrain him. Tina stepped into the small space separating father and son.

Raymond fell back against the doorway, sending the dangling tendrils of bamboo beads into noisy confusion.

Stunned and chastened by the uncharacteristic violence of his own actions, Mr Chun stood stooping slightly. The sound of his laboured breathing interspersed with the dying clatter of the curtain.

As it became clear that he would not hit Raymond again, the tension in the air redirected itself.

'It's those men, isn't it? Don't lie to me again. She saw you talking to them.' His face contorted with anguish, his father continued. 'I told you what would happen if I caught you with them. Don't you know that they're no good? The police know all about them and can't do anything. How do you think they get their money, eh? Honest work? Besides,' he added with a sneer, 'you think money is easy to earn!'

At the mention of his newly acquired 'brothers' and his father's patronising air, Raymond could no longer remain silent. The frustration and unspoken thoughts of his fifteen years were given voice for the first and probably the last time.

'Why do you work so hard! Haven't you got enough money? What's the point? You never spend any of it do you! Look at you – old before your time. You earn all this money and for what? When was the last time you went out for something other than going down the cash-and-carry? When was the last time Mum had the chance to buy a new dress? There's no point is there, because you never go anywhere – YOU'VE GOT NO LIFE!'

Everyone was taken by surprise. Mr Chun stood stunned by Raymond's hometruths. Clearing his throat uneasily he said, 'You think money is easy to earn… ' But he said it without his former conviction. 'This is how we put clothes on your back and fed your miserable face all this time. If we'd stayed in Hong Kong after you were born you wouldn't be getting a good education. You might have… '

'I might have real friends like all the English kids! I wouldn't have complete strangers calling me Chinky and picking on me every time I walk down the street. I'd be able to go out in the evenings like everyone else, not work in the shop all night! You know I'm never going to get anywhere at school; the teachers only notice if you're not there. It's never going to be any different. Don't expect me to take over the shop because I don't want it! I'm not going to spend the rest of my life cooking for people who treat you like scum. Yeah, the money is there, but there are better ways of getting it – ways where you also get respect!'

The outburst left Raymond flushed and breathless. Locked within the heat of the room, the only movement came from a shaft of sunlight glittering with specks of oil being drawn by the extractor fan.

'Respect! You think we enjoy this work? Do you think we had the choice like you have? We don't like it, but we're not ashamed. You think that just because you know English you're better than us and that we know nothing. If you think that this life isn't good enough, then the money isn't either. You know what you can do! Get out now!'

Father and son remained facing each other in silence.

'It's time to open,' Tina said.

Uproar

Paul Wong

It takes an entire morning for my family to prepare for my first trip away from home. My mother packs all my warm clothes in my small blue suitcase. All the hand-knitted jumpers are in there squashed up against each other. I've put some comics in the suitcase too and my slippers: my blue and white rubber flip-flops. My father brings me a box of roast meats to take along: cha siu pork and roast duck wrapped in opaque plastic, sitting smelling sweet in the cardboard box. I'm not nervous, I'm quite blasé in fact. I've always taken things in my stride: what's all the fuss about, I'm only going away for a week. I'm the only child and it's never dawned on me how important I am to my parents.

I carry the box of roasted meats in a carrier bag and take an orange from my mother and put it into a small duffle bag which I sling over my shoulder. My father takes my case to the car. We're going to be late, we're always late. I kiss my mother goodbye. She sheds a tear and her black eyeliner runs. My father drives like a maniac to my school. He swears at the other drivers, calling them white morons and black monkeys, depending on their race. We arrive at the school gates. The coach is waiting. I'm not the only one who's late. I kiss my father goodbye on his fleshy lips, grab my suitcase and run for the coach. I see the other kids looking out from the windows as the driver loads my suitcase into the underbelly of the coach. I keep hold of my duffle bag and the carrier bag with the box of roast meats in it.

There aren't many seats left so I get to sit with the rowdy kids at the back of the coach. I try to be hard and cool, but I look all wrong. My hair doesn't tousle in the right way and I'm just too much of a swot. I end up sitting in the middle space of the back seat of the bus, the one that goes right along the width of the coach, the red and black velour getting hot over the engine. I clutch my bags on my lap, the box of roast meats on top of the duffle bag. The kids around me ignore me and talk about football matches they've been to and their favourite footballers. I've never watched a football match. My father thinks it's a sport for hooligans and Neanderthals, and I believe him. I've seen the crowds of skinheads flooding the street when a match is on.

It's a long coach journey, and I begin to feel a bit ill. My stomach is churning and the heat of the engine is searing into my bottom. I squirm in the seat as the other boys begin tucking into packets of crisps and reading football magazines and boring English comics. My nausea gets worse as the boy on my right starts talking to me, his breath stinking of cheese and onion flavour crisps and cola. He asks me if I'm from Hong Kong, because he knows a boy from the local take-away who was born in Hong Kong. I tell him that I was born in Britain. I guess I must sound really snooty but I really don't want to be associated with those Fried-ricers the Hong Kongers. The boy tells me that this Hong Kong boy is a good footballer. They play on the common at weekends. As he says this he stuffs more crisps into his mouth and then slurps some cola. I feel strange about him telling me this – I've never played football on the common, except with my father or my cousins. Somehow I never really mixed with the other boys.

The boy on my left, Daniel, asks me what I've got in my bags. I tell him it's cha sui pork, my favourite food. He tells me his favourite is macaroni cheese, but I tell him nothing compares to cha sui pork. He asks for a bit, he wants to try some. I like Daniel, he's a rough diamond, he's Jewish and is always talking about his family – how his mother beat him up but how he didn't care and only pretended to cry to make her stop and feel so bad she'd spoil him and give him whatever he wanted. He prefers fighting to football and has a gap in his front teeth, but he's never picked on me. He's always let me be.

I open up the carrier bag and then the box, the sweet barbecue smell explodes in my face and I tear open the plastic and dig out a piece of cold cha sui pork for Daniel. He takes it and chews it. He thinks about it and proclaims it to be not bad. I offer a piece to the cheese and onion kid on my right, and he too approves of a small piece of cha siu pork, saying that he'd tried something similar from his local take-away. Then a boy sitting ahead of me turns around. It's Jan. A small gypsy-ish looking boy, Jan's a tough nut, a hard boy, a bully. He complains about the smell, says it smells like shit and it must be coming from me: 'the chink'. I close the box and tie the handles of the carrier bag into a knot. Daniel yells to Jan that I've got some roast meats, and that they taste really good. Jan swears at Daniel and calls him Jewboy and laughs with his mates. One of the teachers stands up and tells the back of the coach to keep the noise down. The engine heat burns into my backside and I see Jan look round at me and laugh.

We arrive at the camp and I wait until everyone has gone off the coach before I get off. We stand in file and get allocated our huts. The air smells of countryside: slightly damp and green somehow. I carry my suitcase and bags to the hut along with most of the other boys. We put our cases on shelves just before we enter the dormitory. There are two lines of bunk beds and the rest of the boys run to claim their beds near to their friends. I get to share a bunk bed with Paul, a studious and quiet Indian boy. He gets the top bunk and I get the bottom. We're civil to one another, as if we belong to the same club somehow but we haven't ever really talked.

I take out my pyjamas and place them under the pillow and take my new wash bag from my duffle bag, and place it on the bed along with a large orange towel. We've got half an hour before dinner, so I get out my comic books and lie on top of my bed and read them: the X-Men, Superman, The Legion of Super-Heroes. I immerse myself in these brightly coloured panels, where people could fly and everyone was different, had different powers and different costumes but were happy together fighting against common enemies, making a difference. The other boys milled around, larking about, whipping each other with towels and bouncing a football from bed to bed, but I was oblivious to it all.

Dinner comes and goes, I eat the boiled cabbage and the tapioca pudding, thinking about the box of roast meats in my suitcase. After dinner I chat to one of the teachers: Mrs Potts. She's very nice, with long, flame hair and a soft, catlike smile, she's my favourite teacher. I talk to her about what I want to be when I grow up: a doctor, and ask her how difficult it is to become a doctor. I even show off the fact that I know Einstein's formula for relativity: $E = mc^2$, although I get caught out when she asks me to explain it.

It's twilight now and I go back to the hut. I hate the dusk, it always makes me feel depressed. When I enter the dormitory some of Jan's gang are lounging around their beds, they look at me as I enter and they snigger. I look at my suitcase − it's been broken open. I open the lid and find the cha siu pork and roast duck spread all over my clothes and comics. One of the boys can't suppress his laughter anymore and bursts into a hysterical cackle. I march up to him and ask who did it. He tells me it was Jan and points to the next bunk where Jan's jacket is lying on the rough blanket covering the upper bed. Before I know it I've grabbed the mattress and pulled it to the floor. I stamp on the white sheets with my dirty shoes, leaving brown marks and bits of grit all over the starched, bleached cotton. There's a shocked silence from the rest of the boys then the boy who was laughing begins to taunt me: 'You're going to get it − Jan's going to beat the shit out of you now, he's going to fucking kill you.'

I'm holding back the tears and yell 'I don't care', as I leave the dormitory. Jan walks in just as I'm about to leave. I turn

72

and watch him as he walks to his bunk and then sees his overturned mattress. He runs over to me swearing, pointing his finger at me, his face snarling. His finger jabs me in my chest as he asks me why I did what I did to his bed and I begin to retreat further outside the dormitory, stuttering and stammering that he had started it by breaking into my suitcase. The rest of the boys are following us as we move outside onto the entrance to the hut where the electric light blinks on as the light continues to fade from the day. A crowd gathers around us as I'm backed against the railing, Jan's finger still prodding at me, the tears building up behind my eyes which feel like they're ready to burst.

Some of Jan's mates are egging him on, telling him to hit me, to finish me off. Daniel tells Jan to leave me alone, but Jan turns aggressively and warns Daniel to mind his own business, calling him Jewboy again. Daniel shrinks into the crowd and now I've got Jan's full attention again. He starts to slap me across the face, I catch his hand, it's hard and muscular. He pulls it free and tries to slap me with the other hand. I catch his wrist and stop him again. He's shorter than me, he looks like a ferret or a stoat. I can see hate in his eyes as he frees his wrist and there are some boys telling me to hit back, to defend myself. I see Paul looking at me, mouthing the words 'Hit him!', making a fist and swiping the air in front of him. I look at Jan, he throws a punch and once again I intercept it – I catch his fist. Jan yells at me: 'Trying some of that kung fu shit? Can you do karate then?' I feel a tear begin to burst through and then Jan punches me in the mouth. His fist feels numb and cold and as I blink in shock my lips and teeth ache. The next thing I see is Jan's mouth sucking and moving like he was chewing cud. He spits and the saliva hits my face with more force than the punch. My tear ducts explode and I run off, through the crowd, Jan's last words ringing in my ears: 'So much for your Hong Kong phooey karate, you fucking chink.'

A couple of hours had passed since I'd run out of the camp.

I'd seen a few teachers and boys come looking for me with their torchlights and umbrellas. I was moving around from one bus shelter to another, trying to keep out of the rain, trying to stop crying. Eventually, the rain stopped. I was under a tree by the side of the road. I looked up at the dashes of drizzle highlighted under the yellow haze of a nearby streetlight. The tears were coming. My mouth swelled and blubbered uncontrollably. I asked myself why I hadn't fought back, I felt ashamed of myself and told myself to run further, to never go back. How could I face anyone there again? I started to feel cold and thought of my family, of my parents and how they would worry if I disappeared. My courage and my anger melted away and I began to walk back to the camp.

A Question of Debt

Tai Lai Kwan

'Oh no! You've got another dab of paint on your nose!' Carrie was almost doubled up with laughter at the sight of Tom, paper hat askew, paint spattered all over his overall. Her hilarity was highly infectious. Tom took a peep at himself in the hall mirror and couldn't help bursting into laughter as well. He flicked his paint brush at Carrie, and added to the blotches already on her.

They'd been at it the whole morning. There was more paint on themselves than on the walls. It was obvious neither of them had ever painted before. The doorbell interrupted their play. It was Phil. He took one look at Tom and Carrie and screwed up his face.

'You two look a mess!' he pouted.

He took the paint brush away from Tom's hand and threw it to one corner on top of a pile of newspapers and old cloths. 'Don't I get a kiss?' He looked at Tom with a half petulant smile, as he continued to rip paper hat and overall off him.

Tom gave him a peck on the lips, and turned to Carrie with an apologetic nod, 'Sorry Carrie, we'll continue some other time, okay?'

'Sure. You two children go play.' Carrie gave a nonchalant wave at the two receding bodies, arms entwined about each other's waist. She stuck her tongue out at Phil's back.

Carrie tried to continue on her own. After a few haphazard splashdashes she gave up. She had persuaded Tom to start on this renovation. She wanted this to be part of her repayment towards his kindness. At first Tom wouldn't hear of it, 'What quaint ideas you have, Carrie. You've contributed enough. What's all this talk of repaying?'

'Look, it'll just make me feel better, okay. I don't want to

75

have to come back in the next life as your pet dog or something,' Carrie half-jokingly replied. 'Anyway, I'm just offering to pay for half the expenses, you and I still have to do all the work ourselves.'

As it turned out, Tom didn't need much persuasion. He had been meaning to give a new coat of paint to the old apartment and Carrie's wanting to do it was just the impetus he needed. They'd decided to start with the study, the smallest room in the place. Phil's arrival had spoilt her fun.

She enjoyed sharing the house with Tom. She had been there for well over six months now. At first when Tom suggested they marry, she was surprised and touched.

'That's very kind of you Tom. But what about Phil, wouldn't he object? I'll feel like an intruder.'

'Actually I've discussed it with him. He's pretty easy about it. Phil is an independent soul. He has his own pad so you wouldn't really be intruding. He visits frequently of course.'

The offer was irresistible. The marriage would certainly help solve the question of her residency. Two more months and her visa would run out. According to the new immigration laws, she had to return to Hong Kong after the completion of her studies. But, wouldn't she be taking too much of an advantage of Tom?

'So what are friends for? Anyway, you would have to pay lodging and help split the expenses. You would be doing me a favour. The maintenance cost was getting a bit heavy for me.' Then, with the merest hint of mischief in his eyes, he added, 'The old fogies in the street would certainly be bowled by the sight of a woman in the house – and a Chinese one at that!'

Carrie couldn't help smiling at the idea too. Yes, it would certainly give the lace-curtain detectives something to talk about over tea.

Auntie Mary was not convinced at first. 'Who knows what these kwailos have in mind, Carrie! I know he's been your friend throughout college but you can't be too careful,' she warned. She was shocked when Carrie explained Tom was quite safe, because he had a stable relationship with Phil. 'Are you sure you should get involved?' Then her curiosity got the better of her, 'Who's the female between the two?' she asked.

'Oh auntie! Really!' Carrie flashed the whites of her eyes at her Auntie Mary and pointedly ignored her question.

It was finally decided. It's either marriage to Tom, or back to Hong Kong. Auntie Mary agreed it was important for her to obtain residency before 1997 so reluctantly she sanctioned the marriage. In order not to complicate matters, it was also decided that her mother back home should not be burdened with the news. One year was a very short time, and what she did not know, would not hurt her.

Phil had stayed for dinner that night. His fussing over Tom quite put Carrie off her food. But she was careful not to show it. It was her turn to cook that night, and she had prepared Tom's favourite, mainly Szechuan dishes.

Tom was relating a funny incident in the office the previous day. Phil, as usual, was laughing exaggeratedly at every word. Suddenly, his smile froze. Tears welled up in his large, beautiful brown eyes and his features rearranged themselves into a horrified frown as he dropped his fork and spoon and grabbed for his beer. 'AARGH!' He had bitten into a piece of chilli.

Carrie rolled with laughter inside her head. Outwardly, she put on her oh-so-innocent act – her hands flew over her mouth, her eyes wide opened in shock, she cooed, 'Oh Phil, I'm so sorry, I didn't miss a bit of chilli, did I?'

Phil was too busy spluttering into his beer to reply. He did flash Carrie a couple of daggers with his eyes though. He was quite convinced Carrie had left the chilli in on purpose.

'It's all right Carrie, not your fault. He'll be right in a minute.' Tom gave a reassuring smile to Carrie while stroking Phil gently on the back. Dear old Tom, always so trusting, so ready to think the best of everyone.

Of course she did it on purpose. She knew Tom seldom

touched beef dishes, and even if he did, his years of living in Bangkok had developed his taste buds to accommodate chilli well. She just wanted to punish Phil for interrupting her day of painting. Or was it something else. She brushed the thought aside. What else could there be?

The painting job progressed much slower than she had anticipated. With the two of them working, weekends were the only time they had to do it. In between Tom's weekends away with Phil, her own rambling trips, and countless distractions, they only managed two more rooms in a span of six months. She had now been sharing the apartment with Tom for well over a year.

'It shouldn't be too long now before your residency papers come through. You were quite a hit with the immigration officer today you know.'

They were relaxing in the lounge after dinner, re-living the morning's interview yet again.

'I'm just glad it's over. I kept wanting to go to the washroom. I was so afraid he'd ask some intimate questions I couldn't reply.' Carrie rolled her eyes and stuck out her tongue, patting herself over her heart. She was feeling quite euphoric with the success of the interview.

'Our having been college mates together helped. And our field trip to China. He picked me for a sinophile. You certainly conned him with that demure oriental female routine. If only he knew you like I do.' Tom shook his head at Carrie's mischievousness. 'What are your plans now?'

'What do you mean?' Carrie knew what he meant, but was hoping she didn't have to come to it so soon.

'Well, once your residence papers come through, it would be best for you to start separation procedures as soon as possible. You can stay here as long as you like, of course, but I thought you might prefer your own space.'

'Of course. I'll be keeping an eye out for vacant flats around the city. Auntie Mary had said I could move back in with her but I think I'd like to be on my own.' All of a sudden, Carrie didn't feel so bubbly any more. She looked at Tom from under her lashes. He seemed a little worn out.

'Are you still feeling under from your flu?'

'Yes, just a little, this virus does seem to linger on a bit. I'll see the doctor again if it doesn't go away in a few days' time.' Tom appeared rather relaxed about it.

'I think you're just getting old.' Carrie joked. She wasn't worried. Tom generally took good care of himself. In fact, it was Tom who convinced her to cook brown rice instead of white, cut down on oil, salt and sugar and exercise a lot more than she used to, the man was a health fanatic compared to her.

A couple of months went by, Carrie was just going to suggest they should start on the lounge with their repainting when Tom fell ill again.

The apartment was dark as Carrie let herself in – *Strange, Tom should have been home by now.* She turned on the lights and almost jumped out of her skin at the sight of a man sitting in the lounge. It was Tom.

'Tom! You gave me such a fright! What're you doing sitting in the dark?' Carrie saw the look on Tom's face and her belligerence turned into alarm. 'What's wrong, Tom?'

'Come sit down, Carrie. I have something to tell you.' Tom's voice was quiet and grave, otherwise quite normal.

Couldn't be too serious, then. Carrie sat down and waited.

'It has been confirmed. I have AIDS.' Tom said it so matter of factly, it was as if he was just announcing he had cut his hair or something.

Carrie slumped into the couch. She couldn't quite register what she was hearing. She just sat there staring at Tom. In the end, it was Tom who spoke again. 'It would be best for you to move out straight away. You did say your Auntie Mary has a room for you?'

'Yes. But no. I'm not going… Yet. You'll need someone to

take care of you!' Carrie blurted it out.

Tom looked at her, surprised, 'This is no time to play the heroine, Carrie. It's not just a flu, or a fever that I've got.'

Carrie was just about to protest, when the doorbell rang.

'That will be Phil.' Tom got up to open the door.

Carrie got up too, and shut herself away in her room. She couldn't face Phil. She might do something rash like punch him in the face. That would only upset Tom, and he had enough to deal with at the moment. Instinctively she knew Phil had to be the culprit. She knew Phil was no good for him. Tom's other close friends, Mike and Keat, had repeatedly hinted to him that Phil was 'playing the field'. But Tom wouldn't hear of it. Phil had told him he was his only love and Tom believed him. Tom had always been so health conscious. He was not on drugs, he had not been in hospital, and ever since she knew him he had been loyal to Phil. This was so unfair. Why Tom? Anger at the injustice of it all burnt at her innards. A confetti of shreds littered her desk and floor as she sat tearing pieces of writing papers in a blind anger. Tears of frustration were streaking down her face, she was raked with such impotent rage she wished she could pulp Phil there and then.

The front door slammed. Carrie glanced at the clock on her desk. Only half an hour. It sure didn't take Phil long. Normally he would stay the night if ever he came visiting in the evening. Carrie wondered if she should see to Tom and decided against it. He needed to be on his own.

Next day they continued their interrupted conversation. Tom was insistent she move out as soon as possible and Carrie was equally insistent she should stay to keep him company.

'You don't have to do this Carrie. I know you've got this Chinese thing about repaying your debt, but you have been taking care of me all these months. I mean, you've taken over the laundry, the cooking, the vacuuming; we're quits.'

'Don't see why you're so worried. You can't catch AIDS

just through normal contact!'

In the end Tom acquiesced; but he insisted they kept separate sets of crockery and everything had to be scrupulously disinfected. He also confirmed that Phil was the carrier. He thought it only fair that Carrie should know the truth. Mike and Keat were right. Phil had been seeing other people quite freely. What nobody knew was that Phil had been tested HIV positive for some while. What seemed to hurt Tom most was Phil's infidelity. For a while Carrie wasn't sure if Tom was suffering more from AIDS or from a broken heart.

'Hi guys, thanks for coming.' Carrie hugged Mike and Keat in turn. *Why can't I hug Tom the same way?*

'Thank nothing, you silly girl. How's he, still in his room?' Mike gave Carrie an understanding squeeze on the shoulder.

Carrie pointed her chin up the stairs. Mike and Keat gave her a reassuring thumbs up sign as they made their way to Tom.

It's been three weeks since Tom's illness was known. He had given notice at the office and had hardly ventured out except to the clinic. Mike and Keat had been gems. They came round as often as they could. Of Phil, there was no sign.

'We're taking Tom out for a drink, would you like to join us?' The two friends came downstairs, obviously successful in stirring Tom out of his hiding.

'Nah, you guys have a good time.' Carrie felt relieved. Her heart was breaking from the way Tom was wasting away in his head, long before his body was due to break down.

'I'm really worried the way Tom's hiding himself away. I wouldn't have known what to do if you'd not been around as often as you have.'

'Hey, it's okay, kiddo. This is really hard on you, huh?' Mike put his arms round Carrie, marvelling at the way this little lady had stayed by Tom.

'It's not too bad. I just wished he would talk more with me.' Carrie bit back a sniffle, and not wanting to embarrass herself, sought to change the subject: 'have you heard any more of Phil?'

'Nope. Looked like he might have skipped town.' Mike's face darkened at the mention of the name. Phil's irresponsible behaviour had angered all their friends and acquaintances alike. Apparently a few of them had even gone to Phil's apartment to confront him but couldn't find him.

'What about those other people Phil's been seeing? Have they checked out all right?'

'We're not sure…' Mike was about to elaborate when Tom came into the room.

'You joining us, Carrie?' Tom looked at her invitingly. He was washed and spruced up, except for looking a little gaunt, he seemed perfectly normal.

Carrie felt a twinge in her heart. She shook her head. 'Thought I'd catch up with some reading tonight. You guys have fun.' She stifled a sniff as she closed the front door behind them.

•

'You crazy girl. I knew this is not a good idea from the start. Why are you still hanging around. You've got your residency. He's not forcing you to stay, is he?' Auntie Mary was almost incoherent in her hysteria. She was clutching her handbag tight against her chest, eyes darting around the furniture as if she might spot some AIDS germs springing up to latch themselves onto her.

Carrie had not wanted to tell her but Tom was beginning to look really sick. He had lost half his weight, his hair loss had accelerated and his skin was beginning to show the side effects from taking all those pills meant to ease his pain. He had left his job and had spent more and more time at home. Gone were the evenings out drinking with mates; gone was anything that meant having to come into contact socially with anybody. Except for Mike and Keat, he had hardly spoken to anybody.

After a few visits, Auntie Mary had grown suspicious when Tom repeatedly hid in his room instead of being his normal solicitous self to her.

'No, Auntie. Nobody is forcing me to do anything. He needs me now. I just wanted to help.' Carrie couldn't really explain why. She never quite explained it to herself either.

'How am I going to explain all this to your Ma back home? She's bound to blame me. You seeing the doctor?'

'Just don't tell Ma. We've kept everything from her, why start now? I'm quite safe. I'm not truly married to him remember? You can't catch AIDS just being in the same house.' Carrie was trying her best to reassure her aunt, obviously to no effect. Auntie Mary was already edging herself out of the door.

'I'm sorry Carrie. I'm not as brave as you. You'll understand if we don't see each other for a while.' Without even waiting for Carrie's reply, she had jumped into her car and driven off.

As she closed the door, Carrie wondered casually how many tubs of hot water Auntie Mary would use up when she got home.

'I'm sorry Carrie. She's right you know, there's no need for you to hang around. Although I'm really glad you do.'

Carrie turned. Tom was standing by the door to the lounge. He had heard every hysterical word of Auntie Mary's. He looked so pale and frail under the hall light, such a far cry from the healthy, strapping young hunk she knew, that Carrie felt tears welling up inside her. Not wanting Tom to notice, she walked upstairs, away from him, pretending to be angry.

'Don't you start that again. I've had enough of an earful from Auntie tonight.'

•

In the end, all that was left for Carrie to do was to lock up the apartment and leave. She had no intention of keeping the title deed though Tom had insisted. He had called it his payment for the debt he owed her.

'You don't want me to come back as your dog or something, do you?' He'd thrown Carrie's favourite phrase back at her. 'Anyway, you will need the money, there are debts which as my legal spouse you would have to settle. You should have signed the divorce papers, you know.' Tom never understood. He thought it was her Chinese cultural coding which had bound her to the last.

Carrie never quite understood it herself. Maybe it was, maybe it wasn't. She was afraid to probe too deeply within herself.

They never did finish repainting the apartment.

The Casino

K. P. William Cheng

George Orwell is right. Chinese people are addicted to gambling. George Orwell does generalise. But most of the Chinese people I know in Britain like gambling more than they like their own children. They gamble, I suppose, to make a boring life more exciting. They either place their bets on animals like horses and dogs, or on card games like black-jack and banker. During the afternoon when they don't have to work, these Chinese people run down to the local book-maker, and once they finish work at night they change their clothes as quickly as possible and drive to the nearest casino.

•

One such person was Tai Man, also known as Danny. He was introduced to casinos in Britain when he was twenty-one. Ever since then, he had been in love with the smoky atmosphere of a casino in Swansea. It was the nearest betting establishment he could get to. He said that he felt more at home in the casino than he did in the college and in the takeaway, because he could see more Chinese there than he could in the rest of Wales. Besides, he could talk to most of the people there, since their common language was either Cantonese or Hakka.

One night Danny drove to Swansea by himself.

When he entered the casino, he was immediately greeted by a middle aged, bald and repulsive looking Chinese:

'Hi! You okay?' he cried in English.

'Okay.' Danny said. And then in Chinese: 'Fine. fine. You?'

'Same as usual. I have not seen you for a while. What the fuck have you been doing?' he was asked in Cantonese by the same man.

'Busy studying. A lot of homework. Busy in the takeaway. I had no time to gamble. What about you? Have you won?'

'I won fucking nothing. The fucking banker wins all the time. I have fucking lost five hundred pounds.' He could not utter a sentence without an adjective.

'Let's throw dice and be rich.'

They went to the Dice Table and a white man was throwing the dice. Simultaneously people surrounding the table were shouting either 'Two' or 'Twelve' in Cantonese as if they were bargaining in a market. Danny joined in at one corner, placed his bets and waited for the next throw. The white man threw the dice again. One landed with a Three and the other one with a Four. It was Seven. Everybody lost their bet. Danny, as usual, blamed it on the hands of the white man. He muttered in Hakka to the person next to him: 'They do not know how to throw dice.'

The dice fell into the hands of the ugly looking Chinese who swore most of the time. It was his turn. All the bets were placed. He held the dice firmly in his coarse hand, treating them like they were diamonds. Slowly he moved his left hand towards his mouth and blew some air into the tightly closed hand. Very swiftly he threw the dice out. They knocked rhythmically around the high edges of the Dice Table. One dice showed a One and the other showed a Two. A lot of voices were heard at the same time. English, Cantonese and Hakka blended and clashed in the air like nitrogen, oxygen and carbon dioxide mixing with each other in the atmosphere. Danny won thirteen pounds. He seized the opportunity and screamed in English to the dealer: 'Eight Centre! No. Make it Twelve Centre!' The horrible looking middle aged Chinese did what he did the first time with the dice. What a gesture. The dice were thrown after this dramatic act. It was a Two. Danny won nearly a hundred pounds. He could not believe his luck, and screamed across to the bald man in Cantonese: 'You really have the hands of God like Maradona!'

Danny increased his bets. He won more. In half an hour he won nearly three hundred pounds.

He then turned to the Black-Jack Table. Luck seemed to drift away from him. He gradually lost what he had won. After losing a couple of games, he doubled and tripled his bets. He put sixty pounds on the betting box and was given a King and a Queen. The dealer had a Five on the table. It was a pretty bad start and Danny thought that this time, with his twenty points, he could win some money back.

The dealer inquired of every gambler whether they wanted any card, but no one said yes. Not even the Chinese woman who had a Jack and a three wanted to risk the precious chance of waiting for the dealer to bust. So it was the dealer's turn to draw his cards. Simultaneously the Chinese people were screaming in English:

Picture!

Picture!

As predicted the dealer obtained a Jack. So he had to draw another card. When he moved his hand to the card box, the Chinese people, almost like a witch-hunt, yelled again in English:

Picture!

Picture!

It was an Ace. Another card was required. The cry of 'Picture! Picture!' was louder and louder. It was as though they were protesting outside Parliament. The dealer drew the card and when it was exposed to naked eyes the shocked faces looked like they had just experienced an earthquake. No one could believe what they saw, and the dealer began to collect the bets. Everybody on the Black-Jack Table shouted in Cantonese: *'Yau Mo Kau Chaw'* (Is there anything wrong?).

The longer Danny stayed in the casino, the more he lost of what he had won earlier on. In fact he was starting to lose the three hundred pounds he'd brought with him.

He decided to move to the Roulette Table with his remaining two hundred pounds. He changed half of his money into blue chips. Blue had always been his lucky colour. So he said. He scattered the chips on the thirty-seven numbered squares, with a heavier portion on the lower end. At the same time the little silver ball was travelling speedily around the rim of the roulette like a man-made satellite running around the Earth. Some thirty seconds later it looked as though the satellite gradually hit the Earth surface and the tiny pieces were jumping about on the ground. finally the silver ball rested itself on the number 24, and someone was screaming like mad. It was not Danny. He only had one chip on that winning square, but a Chinese woman who stood next to him had a dozen chips on Square Box 24. She was jubilant. Danny was dejected. So with not many blue chips he placed his bet again hoping that this time he could win back the loss. The same process began. The tiny silver ball rolled around the rim of the roulette again. It was endless, like the Earth going round the Sun. The movement of the ball slowed down gradually and hit the centre of the roulette. It jumped and jumped until eventually it found its home on the number 0. A lot of voices were heard. Tai Man was screaming like mad this time. But it was a cry of self-pity instead of triumph. Damn. He had put all the remaining chips almost everywhere on the betting table, but the box 0 was a little too far for him to reach. He won nothing. He lost two-thirds of his money.

Grumbling in Cantonese: 'I have nearly lost all my money', he teamed up with the gruesome-looking Chinese man again and went to the Dice Table. His friend said to him in Hakka: 'What? Lost all the fucking money? Always chance to win when there is a gamble. Continue.'

They occupied two spaces which were directly facing the dealers. An old Chinese man of mid-sixty held the dice and was ready to throw.

'Twelve.' announced one of the dealers.

Danny mumbled in English: 'Just my luck. Should've come ten seconds earlier and shouted "Four Centre".' He began to place his bet. So did the horrible-looking, bald Chinese man.

Without performing any ritual like the bald one did, the old man threw his dice. 'Seven' announced the dealer.

It was Danny's turn to throw. He believed in himself. So he doubled his bet. His friend told him: 'Throw good.' The dice danced on the table, going round and round, like a female ballet dancer twirling her attractive body. Two Twos faced up and Danny said in English: 'Thank God.' He threw again and the dice danced again. Two Threes were seen. Danny was pleased. So he quadrupled his bet. His friend saw what he did and said to him: 'You are ferocious. It is like you are fucking betting all you have!' Danny grinned and did not respond. He had faith in himself. The dice were thrown out of Danny's hand. This time they knocked on the table more rhythmically than any other time. One dice stopped and showed a Five. Everyone was waiting for the other dice to stop twirling. They were shouting too.

Five!

Five!

The movement of the whirling dice was almost echoed by the heartbeats of the participants.

Five!

Five!

The dice was like a little doll dancing to a music box. It twirled and twirled. Tai Man fixed his eyes on this spinning dice. His head spinned too. He felt slightly giddy.

Five!

Six!

The dice stopped all of a sudden.

'Seven,' announced the dealer.

'Fuck the cunt of your mother!' cried the ugly Chinese man in Cantonese.

'*Yau Mo Kau Chaw!*' yelled Danny.

Without uttering another word Tai Man headed to the entrance. He had only twenty pounds left. He was in a bad mood. It was half past three in the morning. He drove back to Fishguard at seventy miles per hour.

Snapshots of a Girl's Life

Tracy Cheung

This time I am gonna really kill him. Not just slap him around a little, but honest to goodness kill the smarmy, hateful beast. All blond hair, blue eyes and innocence on the outside, but inside, all bitter and twisted spite. Out in the yard, I braced myself for battle – I would show no mercy. He was a couple of years younger than I actually was – a legacy from my poor, short parents. It was something that infuriated me, but despite the humiliation of being challenged by a mere seven year old, I was going to kill this sorry boy and show the school just how strong I was!

He came skipping into the yard, curly locks all a-bouncing. How I longed to rip off that cute, curly head. I smiled to myself. 'I'll show you what bloody "Monkey Magic" is all about.' I grimaced, remembering how he'd got the others to shriek the TV theme tune to me. Horrible, horrible sound, that rang in my ears. All that funny talk those Chinese people spoke in the programme. I knew I didn't speak like that, though sometimes my parents did. Even so, they didn't quite sound like those dubbed voices the white actors imagined Chinese people sounded like. I had hurt, a funny, painful feeling. I took a deep breath and broke out into a run, my fist at the ready. 'Chippy Taka, *this!*'

•

One summer, things started changing. The girls in my secondary school got taller and more willowy, whilst I remained short and, I thought to myself, not as beautiful. My best friends, Sarah and Clare suddenly got breasts. I acquired unmomentous bumps. Suddenly, the changing rooms at games became a nightmare for those who hid in towels and still wore vests. The girls who wore lacy bras – and actually had something to fill them with – became cool and sophisticated. Some girls just faded away into the background, hating their bodies. I developed a good line in scowling and jokes at the expense of those who weren't careful.

The thing was, I felt foolish but I didn't want to advertise the fact. I despaired of my looks and hid myself in long, baggy clothes. My two friends, Sarah and Clare were not the coolest kids, but passed as reasonably cool, and their standing in the year rubbed off on me. Nevertheless, I would step apart even from them, as if the truth about who I was might be too horrible to contemplate.

Boys made the whole situation worse. All of a sudden, it seemed, I discovered that they had a purpose other than to slap around and play rounders with. We were meant to make them *like* us!

Clare was the first of us to get a boyfriend. We were on a school holiday, a week in Yorkshire, no parents, just a couple of hip teachers and twenty-five fourteen year olds. I was in heaven! My parents were not as liberal as my friends' and I had only ten pounds spending money, and some coins to phone home with; but there I was, sharing a chalet with my two best friends. It was 1979, the year the summer seemed to last forever.

'Faye, do it again!'

Sarah and Clare were laughing as we ran along the Pennines in warm June sunshine. I was laughing so hard my stomach was hurting. 'No, I can't!' I cried.

'Go on!' yelped Sarah, 'that's so funny, I'm gonna tell Mr Stevens you can do him if you don't!'

'I can only do it when I concentrate!' I protested, still spluttering with laughter. Sometimes, if I was in the mood I could relax my face and squeeze it into a character but often it was spontaneous and I couldn't repeat it. Mr Stevens was a real liberal type lefty drama teacher, who tried to be cool but more often than not missed the mark. I wrinkled my nose and leaned my head to one side. 'So, tell me, Sarah, when you say you hate your mother, do you think you are really saying that you hate yourself?'

Sarah and Clare shrieked again. I fell on them, convulsed with laughter. 'Don't make me do it again,' I begged, 'or I'll bust my guts.'

The sound of male laughter made us swing around suddenly. We kept giggling and I was pleased I had an appreciative audience. The tall boy with dark hair smiled at me and I felt this *leap* inside, quite catching me out. 'Pull yourself together,' I commanded myself silently. Two of the boys whispered together.

'Are you lot going to the disco tonight?' the tall one asked, directing his question at us collectively.

'Yeah, what time is it starting?' Clare asked, Ms Supercool to the end.

The boy in the checked shirt and red hair shrugged and looked at his friends. 'I think we'll be there about eight.'

'Maybe we'll see you there,' Clare said nonchalantly. She linked arms with both Sarah and me. 'Come on girls. See you later on.'

'Okay.' the tall one said.

As we walked away, Sarah leaned forward in glee.

'One each! And they're older!'

'What are their names?' Clare giggled. I let out an excited laugh.

'We'll find out.' Sarah declared.

•

The disco was a small affair. The dining room had the tables and chairs pulled back and fairy lights adorned the wall. There was a small record and tape deck and a bar serving non-alcoholic punch or coke. Sarah and Clare had managed to find dresses in their rucksacks and I had a long, black satin shirt I wore over my jeans. I scorned at their dresses but they pulled faces at me, knowing I didn't really care what they wore.

One part of me demanded that I had better not hope for

too much and another wanted something, I don't know what, to happen. I looked in the chalet mirror before we came out, when Sarah and Clare weren't looking. My hair was shiny black in the light. I strained forward to peer at my face. I was always disappointed. Clare had fantastic cheek bones. My face was smooth and clear but I didn't have those hollows I liked so much. My nose always let me down. I had almost no bridge and I'd always wanted a perky little nose with narrow nostrils instead of a flat bob. My eyes that were so like my mother's, I thought they looked fine on Mahmee but on me they just didn't sit quite right.

When Sarah and Clare tried to make me up once, they tried to apply eyeshadow with ridiculous results.

'Your lids are really funny!' Sarah mused, frowning. 'I can't get them right.'

'Here, let me have a go.' Clare suggested.

I shook my head, rubbing the Rimmel shadow off with my fingers. 'No, I don't want to. Let me do you instead.'

'Okay.' Clare said.

I applied the shadow to Clare's eyelids carefully. Her eyelids rolled back into her eye sockets and were a great canvas to make shadows on, like how they demonstrated on the Beauty pages of *Jackie* and *Blue Jeans* magazines. Why couldn't I make myself look like that? I stared at Clare's eyes, fascinated. My eyelids were creases in the skin, I couldn't make shadows in the socket bone like Clare or Sarah could. I couldn't figure it out, why was my face so unyielding to make up? *Jackie* didn't feature eyes that looked like mine, perhaps that has something to do with it? Mahmee never wore makeup, so I never saw how to do it properly.

Whilst I peered at myself in the chalet mirror, I prayed to God that I wouldn't get the ugly boy – the one with the ginger hair. I allowed myself just a quick thought of the dark-haired boy called Stephen, before I pushed him out of my mind and ran out of the chalet to join Sarah and Clare.

Clare snogged Stephen at nine-thirty outside the disco.

Sarah danced with his fair-haired friend James and I ignored the ginger-headed boy, who got bored and eventually went back to his chalet.

I cried that night, silently in my bunk so as not to wake the girls up. I was pleased for Clare of course, but he'd smiled at me, *I* was the one who'd got us talking! There was something wrong with me, or, at least, something that set me apart from the others. I didn't rate Sarah as being cleverer or prettier than me, but I was *different*. I was witty and sharp, but it wasn't enough. Perhaps if I'd been born blonde and white my whole life might have led quite a different course. Inside, I knew there was someone waiting to burst out and take on the world, someone who was valuable, someone only a few people came close to seeing. No-one saw beyond my young, flat, Chinese face.

.

When I was sixteen, I met a girl. She was smart, she was street-wise and she was black. I'd never met anyone like Marcia before. The girl had attitude and I thought she was the coolest. Sarah and Clare were a bit put out when I started to hang out with Marcia, but I didn't care, because they had started drifting away from me and towards each other. Marcia and I had this understanding. We didn't have to speak about it, it just *was*.

Marcia talked about her blackness a lot. She loved being black because it was cool and she had respect because of it. Girls didn't mess with her, they were too frightened, but she wasn't the kind to go hitting people, even though she spoke about it. Her reputation went before her and Marcia just took advantage of it. I even started thinking how I would like to be black, because of the instant street credibility. Somehow, Chinese people didn't have that cool factor at school, generally speaking.

I used to go to Marcia's house and listen to her records all day. Her whole family was kind of cool, I thought. I learned a lot being around Marcia, she dared to be different and she liked being loud. Marcia knew who I was, and slowly, I came to know who I was too.

Snowdrop

Mei Chi Chan

She had come to tell them of her decision.

Standing by the door of the kitchen in the semi-darkness, a faint odour of bleach and onions greeted her like an old and comfortable companion. Silence, condensed by the hum of the refrigerators, echoed through and drew her in.

The florescent strips flickered before exploding off the hard, sharp surfaces, pricking out the edges, threatening the shadows. This was a kitchen that spoke not of home and its comforts but of forges, armoury and battle. For now, the steel rested. The oil in the deep fryer was cool, brown and thick as treacle. The heavy iron range stood dominating the room like an altar; the four holes cut side by side into its black metal looked curiously vulnerable to her, and she resisted the temptation to cover them up with the woks that huddled upside down like turtles beneath the range.

She walked across the room to the chopping board that stood on its own. Knives and choppers of different shapes and sizes hung from one of its edges, resembling a set of monstrous teeth. She could almost hear the thud of a heavy blade cleaving through flesh and bone onto the wood below. Delicately, she traced the scars on the surface. Tiny fragments of wood tickled her fingertips. In two hours her mother would come down the stairs and enter this arena. The fires would be lit, the oil would begin to bubble and steam and the steel would start to clash. She remembered Friday nights when she was a child. Friday was the busiest night of the week. People invaded the take-away in hordes after the pubs had closed. Reeking of cigarette smoke and with the sour smell of drink on their breath, they demanded to be fed. Inside the kitchen she would sit, unable to help: the still centre in the madly spinning wheel of movement around her. She would look backwards and forwards between her father and her mother. Their faces frightened her, she could not recognise them. They were not their daytime selves, they became something impersonal, mechanical, and even monstrous. They were like the knives, slashing, paring, chopping, slicing, dividing. Moving through the thick greasy white smoke like the warriors of old, advancing in the mists of dawn; they looked invincible. Every ounce of being was consumed in the task of making food. It could not be called 'cooking'. Cooking sounded too homely. No, like alchemists, they brought forth food out of steel and fire. Their creations subdued and sated the hungry hordes that bayed impatiently outside.

She walked over and bent down to pick up one of the steel woks beneath the range. She tested it for its weight, savouring the way it felt to grip the wooden handle in her hand and the tension stretching her wrist. She dropped it onto one of the holes and it made a dull clunk as it landed. She walked round and round the kitchen, circling the aluminum worktop that was the centrepiece of the room. At times, she would stride, eyes wide and blazing. Then at other times her steps turned into a shuffle. She sighed and muttered, shaking her head: *I can't, I can't do it, I can't, I really can't. They can. But not me. I'm too soft, too weak, too split. I don't have it – what it takes. I – will – fail.*

But there was another voice in her head, saying: *you can, you can do it. Of course you can. You have had the training. You have the guts. You have stamina. That's all you need. The rest will take care of itself.* She heard footsteps. She felt a shaking in the depths of her stomach. They would ask her and she would not know what to say…

•

'Snowdrop. That's a snowdrop.' The little girl listened deeply to the word. Gem-like, it sank into her heart and made it glow. A blue-green stem, a slender arch over virginal snow, and a white pendant flower dangling like an echo over it. 'A snowdrop.' That first, never-ending winter in England. Frosted air that bit her lungs, toes that never thawed, strangers made stranger still, wrapped and hunched and invisible in their layers, voices that blew like gusts into her ears, sound without meaning – until the word 'snowdrop'. Something melted. It was the feeling that she could not express then, the feeling of a fragile white flower rising over the snow. Now she would call it 'hope'. How thankful she was not to have known the word then.

They would ask her and she would say 'snowdrop' and they would understand. The word would turn like a key in their hearts. Snowdrop, snow-drop, a flower, a drop of…

Her mother and father broke into the space and light. She looked at them for a moment and there was confusion. In her mind they had been giants. Had they always been so small? How sallow and faded they looked, like parchment. In an instant, doubt vanished, and the two voices in her head united: *They cannot win. I will not be able to win here either. It is the wood, the metal, the blades, the oil, the flames – that last. It is the flesh and the spirit that are bowed and twisted for their purpose. Those warriors of myth and legend were invincible only in stories. Blood is spilt, flesh and bone are torn and shattered and burnt. Only the weapons remain unharmed: wood and metal gleaming as though smiling. The victory belongs to them. All the while we feared the hordes beyond; all the while they were among us here. And my parents, what is left of them?*

When she spoke, her voice was steady and clear. And when she told them that she would not stay and work in the kitchen they did not try to persuade her. Her father turned on the fryer and her mother lit the range.

Discovery

Graham Chan

Most people never realised I had a brother. When I was asked, I didn't actually lie, but I was sufficiently uncommunicative as to discourage further questions. After all, it would be embarrassing to have to explain to English people that we were estranged from my brother because he had married one of them. I had learned long ago to be careful what I said to white people; even with my closest friends, I knew there were some things they would never be able to understand or accept, and it was safer not to talk about them at all.

When his daughter was born, I visited them secretly, not wanting to risk my parents' wrath. The atmosphere was relaxed though a little uncertain in the way it always is when you visit someone's house for the first time. I could have done without the folk music, but at least we were able to joke about it. They were members of a local folk club, and thinking it would be a pleasant evening's entertainment for us all, they took me there. We listened to a young man chanting in the obligatory, fake Wessex accent about fields of corn and maidens fair, and to my horror we were all expected to join in the chorus. I was trying hard to be an obliging guest but this was too much, and I kept my mouth stubbornly closed.

'This isn't your cup of tea, is it?' asked Sandra, my sister-in-law.

'No, I'm afraid not, but don't worry. We can stay as long as you like. I'll pretend I'm fresh off the boat and can't speak English.'

'That might get you into even deeper water. They'll probably invite you to sing some Chinese folk songs. We'd better go to the pub.'

There was only one awkward moment, when we were

sitting at the dinner-table and the built-up hurt and resentment seemed to overflow. Sandra suddenly turned to me and asked aggressively:

'What's it like to have no family?'

'What do you mean?'

'Well, you're not like other people. Everyone else has brothers and sisters and uncles and aunts and cousins all around them. I see my family nearly every day, we're in and out of each others' houses all the time. But you don't have anyone. It must be horrible.'

'I have my parents and my sister.'

'That's not a family!'

'It's all I have. Of course we have aunts and uncles that we see sometimes, but no one lives near us, so we don't see them very often.'

'But it's not normal. I can't understand how anyone could live like that.'

I wasn't sure whether she really was obliquely complaining about the way we had treated her and my brother, or whether she was simply defining normality as being her way of life, her beliefs, her likes and dislikes. Anyway, I knew we were on dangerous ground, so I just said:

'It's the way it's always been; we're used to it.'

I was on the point of saying something about us being immigrants and so not having the luxury of growing up surrounded by friends and relatives like Sandra, but fortunately, at that moment the baby began to whimper, so both Sandra and my brother jumped up to look after her.

Sandra picked her up and lulled her back to sleep, then she turned to me and placed her in my arms, saying:

'You can hold her for a while.'

I was terrified. She was so tiny and fragile, I felt as though if I moved a single muscle I must inevitably crush her out of existence. Wrapped up in blankets like a weightless parcel and with her eyes closed, she evinced no detectable signs of life. I could not even hear her breathing and was panic struck at the thought that she must have died just as Sandra was handing her over to me.

'She's so small. Is she alright?' I asked hesitantly.

My brother laughed.

'We were like that at first. Every few minutes we were looking at her and asking each other if she was still breathing.'

'You'd better take her,' I said, 'I'm afraid I'll drop her.'

'You're doing alright, just relax. You should get some practice at this while you can. It might come in handy when you've got some of your own.'

'No thanks. I don't want any children – horrible, noisy things.'

I passed the baby back to my brother.

'She is beautiful though,' I said.

Over the next few years I watched and marvelled as she grew more and more beautiful. I told my parents about my visit. My mother didn't want to know anything about them, but she said if I wanted to see them, that was up to me. My father asked if they seemed happy, and when I said 'yes', he simply nodded. After that I visited them once a year, becoming the uncle who always brought Margaret some fabulous old toys, survivors of our own childhood: a doll's house that our grandmother made out of cardboard and wallpaper, the blue teddy-bear that my sister used to sleep with, the plastic farmyard animals which had been packed away unused in the attic for so long that my brother had to spend hours cleaning and repairing them before he could give them to Margaret.

•

I have to say, though, that my visits were made out of a sense of duty rather than affection. As my brother's life seemingly settled into a reasonably prosperous and well-deserved contentment, I felt less and less affinity for him. He was so well-integrated into his local community, he had so many articulate, university-educated friends, he had so many relatives (albeit all Sandra's) around him, he was so English, that I began to feel out of place in his house and struggled to find anything to talk about, or at least anything non-controversial. I always had to be careful to avoid any topic of conversation that might lead to a major row with Sandra: politics, society, race relations, the government, the workers, the environment, human rights, nuclear disarmament, children, dogs (when they briefly acquired one, I told them I couldn't visit them any more; Sandra couldn't understand this, she couldn't understand how anyone could not like dogs). I knew they were better people than I was: more generous, more committed, more caring, but to me the causes they supported so passionately were for white people who, if the chips were down, would abandon us to the mob. I found it difficult to conceal my contempt when they told me they were canvassing for the Labour Party. Sandra, of course, could not know what our experience of the British working class had been, but had my brother forgotten the daily insults and catcalls, the times we had been spat at or beaten up, the routine smashing of the restaurant windows, the constant clamour for compulsory repatriation if not extermination? Why was he now supporting the people who wanted to kill us?

Perhaps I would have felt differently if my own life had not been dissolving into chaos, if I too had found an English girl to settle down with. Anyway, he was still my brother, and I like to think that maybe my alienation at least played some part in healing the breach in our family. As I took to spending more and more time abroad, working on short-term jobs in obscure tropical backwaters and trying to convince myself that it was better than living in England, I guess my parents began to feel the emptiness of their house. My mother never asked me anything about my brother, but after each of my visits my father would want to be reassured that they were happy and that Margaret was alright.

One year, my brother gave me a photograph of himself

and Sandra sitting on the sofa with Margaret nestling between them. When I showed it to my father, he muttered something in Cantonese which I didn't understand; much later I found out that it meant: 'how beautiful!' Eventually, he must have decided, without saying anything to anybody, that this had gone on long enough and it was time to put an end to it. He summoned my brother, telling him to bring his family for a visit. My brother was understandably reluctant to risk exposing his family to any further unpleasantness, but a direct order from our father could not possibly be disobeyed, so in the summer they came.

We needn't have worried. It took only a few minutes for Margaret to melt our parents' reserve and make the years of bitterness fade away. By this time, Margaret was five years old and it was impossible not to love her. She had the breathtaking, delicate beauty that you often see in children of mixed marriages, as well as the classic Chinese, luxurious, glossy black hair flowing over her shoulders. But more than that, she was sweet-natured and gentle and affectionate. My brother sometimes called her Petal, and the name was exactly right.

•

But as my brother and I sat in the kitchen drinking coffee while Sandra and our mother rearranged the bedrooms upstairs, speaking to each other warily and ultra-politely, Margaret came in with a puzzled frown on her face.

'There's a strange man in the other room, come and look,' she said, taking my hand and pulling me towards the door.

'He's not a strange man,' I replied, 'he's your Grandpa.'

'No, he's not!' she exclaimed. 'I know who my Grandpa is!'

'So who is your Grandpa?'

She was starting to get exasperated at my stupidity.

'You know! You've met him: Grandpa Henry, he lives just near us with Nanna Jean.'

'They're your Mummy's Mum and Dad. The man in the other room is your Daddy's Dad.'

'I didn't know Daddy had a Dad.'

'Everyone does, everyone has a Mum and a Dad.'

'But he can't be Daddy's Dad. He looks funny, and he doesn't speak properly.'

'That's because he's not English. He comes from another country, where they speak a different language, so he had to learn English in school and he can't speak it as well as you can.'

'What country does he come from?'

'China.'

'But if he's Daddy's Dad, he must be your Dad as well. But if he comes from another country, he can't be. You and Daddy are both English.'

I was starting to feel my brother ought to take over this exhausting explanation, but he seemed content to let me flounder on while he sat and listened with an amused smile on his face.

'Our Dad was born in China, so he's Chinese, but he came to England a long time ago, before your Daddy and I were born, so we were born here.'

Her frown was very deep now; she was having to think very hard.

'My Mummy's not Chinese; she's English, isn't she?'

'Yes.'

'So what are you and Daddy: Chinese or English?'

'We're both.'

She laid her head in my lap and digested this for a minute or so. Then she asked, hesitantly:

'Does that mean I'm Chinese too?'

'Yes, you're like me and Daddy. You're Chinese and English at the same time.'

'Is that why some people don't like me?'

My brother's smile disappeared abruptly. Before I could reply, he leaned forward and asked:

'Why do you think they don't like you?'

'They call me names sometimes.'

'That's because they don't know you. If they knew you, they would like you. Don't take any notice of them. As long as you're being a good girl, that's all that matters.'

'Alright. If they don't want to be friends, I don't mind. I have lots of friends already. But where is China?'

'Why not ask your Grandpa? Ask him to show you some pictures.'

'Alright.'

She rushed off enthusiastically like all children do when they discover an interesting new task to perform.

My brother and I looked at each other.

'She had to find out sometime,' I said.

'I suppose so, but I always hoped somehow it would never happen to her.'

'If she can handle it like you do, she'll be okay. It never seems to bother you, you just take it in your stride, but it makes my blood boil every time.'

'It's no use letting it poison your life or hating people because of it. We have to live here, so we'd better make the best of it. It's our country as much as anyone's, and unless we treat it as ours, we'll always be outsiders.'

'I've never felt this was my country. I don't think I ever will.'

'So where is your country? Don't kid yourself that it's China or Hong Kong. We may look the same as those people but inside we're completely different. We'd be just as out of place there as here, maybe even more so.'

'I know. I had to tell Margaret we're Chinese but really I don't know what we are. All I know is, it sticks in my throat to say I'm English.'

My brother smiled again.

'And so it should,' he said, 'seeing as how you were born in Scotland. Come on, let's go and see how Dad's getting on with Margaret.'

Margaret was gazing in silent wonder at a photograph of two skinny boys wearing bathing trunks and floppy, white sun hats, sitting in a rock pool and holding Coca-Cola bottles in their hands. It was a photograph that had always fascinated me too, because I had no recollection of that day near Shatin, Hong Kong New Territories, no recollection except for the delicious taste of the Coca-Cola.

That summer when my brother and his family visited us was Britain's hottest on record. It was so hot that for the one and only time, my mother's peach tree blossomed and bore fruit: big, luscious, juicy peaches. My father seemed to go nuts.

'I don't know what's come over your Dad,' my mother said. 'Every day he's out there drooling over the peaches. You know he's never done anything in the garden before, but he put a net over them to keep the birds off and he's constantly taking photographs of them. Look at him now with Margaret.'

My father had set up his ancient camera on a tripod and was positioning Margaret amongst the branches of the peach tree, turning her head and her hands this way and that, taking photograph after photograph. She certainly made a beautiful picture, but for my father there seemed to be more to it than that.

'Look at that camera,' I said, laughing, 'why on earth did he dig that out when he's got a brand-new one sitting in his wardrobe?'

'He brought that camera with him from Hong Kong,' my mother said, 'amazing it still works.'

And I stopped laughing, because I suddenly remembered the traditional Chinese paintings of children playing under the peach trees, and I understood that all this, the peaches, the camera, and the beautiful grandchild, had something to do with being Chinese. My father was happy in a way I had never seen before: the child he had thought was lost had been found again, and, as she herself had just discovered, she was Chinese after all. The past was finished, but the future would continue, and the camera was there to record both. How ironic that it was my brother who had brought all this about. My brother, who had become so English, had yet brought a Chinese happiness to my father.

Biographies

Graham Chan

Graham Chan is a librarian. He was born in Scotland and has travelled widely, but has never felt he belonged anywhere. As he only speaks a few words of Cantonese, the only place he has felt completely comfortable is Singapore, because most people there are Chinese but speak English.

Mei Chi Chan

Origin unknown. Psycho-physical components from Hong Kong, Nigeria, England and Taiwan. Degree-ed in Philosophy, careered as a teacher, textbook writer (Taiwan) and literature officer (Liverpool). Married and un-married. De-careered. Lived in monasteries in England. Presently teaching and practising meditation in a Thai Buddhist nunnery. Destination blissfully unknown.

K. P. William Cheng

Twenty-six year old K. P. William Cheng was born in Hong Kong but educated in England. As an English Literature graduate, he writes short stories and poems for pleasure. In most cases his work reflects his life experiences. He now works and lives in Hong Kong as a Travel Consultant, and is still writing.

Tracy Cheung

Tracy Cheung was born in London. She is a Housing Officer by day and a sometime scribbler with high hopes. This is her second published work. She is currently working on a longer term project drawing on family and social history, memory and creative imagination. Her ambition is to produce a full length novel.

Hi Ching

Born in London but spending my childhood in Singapore, I started out as a dancer, became an actor, diversified, ran a dance school and company, began to write and continued to diversify. As a result, I ended up artistic director of Continuum Arts organising Chinese arts events and projects.

Deniell Rebecca J. Lawrie

My parents fled the communist war – my mother was just nineteen years old – to a country paved with gold, or so she was told. I was born and raised in the heart of an ever-changing Liverpool, the youngest of six children. Future? I continue to travel and write.

D. K .Y. Lee

D.K.Y. Lee was born in England 1966, went to school in Southampton and studied History at London University. Lawyer and failed Yuppie, she later gained a Masters degree, obtaining a scholarship for research in China on the way. Generally lives in London with a goldfish. Hopes to finish something one day.

Florence Li

My name is Florence Li, 李鐵康 (meaning to have Iron Health, and if you ask nicely, I'll tell you how I came to acquire this name). I am twenty years old and currently studying for a Psychology degree at Manchester University. Writing for me has come about accidentally. I hope that I come across to my audience like some young, clued up, sassy, cute babe (huh, I wish!).

Dedication: To my paternal grandad, Jennifer and Jimmy Yeung – who were my initial inspiration for *Journal*. All my love and thanks to my parents who have been really supportive and William Cheung.

Tai Lai Kwan

Other people move homes. I move countries. Ever since my parents uprooted themselves from China, I've kept myself moving: from Malaysia to Australia, then Singapore, UK, now back to Singapore again. Am I finally settling down? I hope not. Far too many countries to explore, people to know. In tandem with my physical migration, my life stages have also evolved from zealous social worker to high powered executive to now? Professional hedonist.

Daniel Wong

Daniel was born in Hong Kong, works as a waiter and writer, and lives in London with his male partner.

Paul Wong

My overseas Chinese parents left their native tropical paradises to come to the greyness of Britain to study. In between exams they met, fell in love and got married. At twenty past midnight on Saturday the seventh of March 1964, I was born in the Queen Mother's Hospital, Glasgow. The rest is history.

Commonword

Commonword develops, supports and publishes new writing in the North West, and in particular creates opportunities and access for groups who are under-represented in the field of writing and publishing. The organisation facilitates writers' workshops, runs courses, holds public readings and events and gives advice and information to groups and individuals on all aspects of writing and publishing.

Established in 1977 as a unique regional resource, Commonword is a not-for-profit organisation operating under community co-operative rules.

Cultureword

As a centre for black creative writing, Cultureword has achieved singular success in discovering, developing and promoting black writers. Cultureword organises black writers' workshops, poetry performances, residencies and training events.

Crocus

Crocus is the publishing imprint of Commonword and Cultureword and has established a reputation for fresh, innovative work. Crocus produces collections of poetry and short stories, and novels, which are distributed nationally.

Commonword is supported by: The Association of Greater Manchester Authorities, North West Arts Board and Manchester City Council's Central Grants Team.

Recent Crocus Titles

No Limits

A collection of sixteen stories about city life delivering a rich cast of characters in crisp, incisive and often witty writing.

'The short story is alive and well and living in Manchester.'
(City Life)
ISBN 0 946 745 26 9
£6.50 Pbk

Kiss

A vivid collection of modern love poetry by Asian, African and Chinese writers. By turns tender, political and sensuous, this book single-handedly takes love poetry into the twenty-first century.

'These pieces of work are a testimony to the fact that our humanity, despite efforts to distort and destroy it, will always take priority.' (Martin Glynn)
ISBN 0 946745 21 8
£5.95 Pbk

Looking for Trouble
Cath Staincliffe

She's a single parent. A private eye. And liking it. Until, that is, Mrs. Hobbs turns up asking Sal Kilkenny to find her missing son…

'With a cast of characters drawn from the gutter to the high ranks of business and officialdom, she probes the city's underbelly in an exciting tale of corruption, exploitation and brutality.'
(Val McDermid)
ISBN 0 946745 31 5
£5.95 Pbk

Talkers Through Dream Doors

Fourteen talented Black women write about their lives in this collection of poetry and short stories.

'These voices reassert the Black identity and cross new boundaries to redefine it.' (Amrit Wilson)

ISBN 0 946745 60 9

£3.95 Pbk

Crocus Five Women Poets

A showcase of poetry by Barbara Bentley, Marguerite Gazeley, Francis Nagle, Sheila Parry and Pat Winslow. These five women are quickly emerging as some of the most talented poets in recent years.

'Here are poems that tackle everything from domestic chores to international politics with grace, wit and assurance.' (City Life)

ISBN 0 946745 16 1

£5.95 Pbk

Flame

A dual language book of poetry in English and Urdu by Asian writers. Love, home life, racism are some of the areas explored by the fifteen talented poets. Translations by Alishan Zaidi.

'One of the best collections of Asian poetry I have read.' (Eastern Eye)

ISBN 0 946745 85 4

£4.50 Pbk

Crocus Debuts

A series of pamphlets launching new and diverse voices.

Art is Only a Boy's Name

Liz Almond

Liz Almond's poetry explores ambiguity; the coexistence of opposites – she has a painter's eye, H. G. Well's sense of time and a word lover's passion about language.

'The poems have a quiet confidence... this doesn't feel like a first collection.' (10th Muse)

ISBN 0 946745 36 6

£2.50 Pbk

Regrouting the Bathroom in the 21st Century

Alan Peat

Poetry which applauds difference and travels to find it. Much of Alan Peat's poetry is written while traveling and has a strong sense of place, whether of a Durham pit village, a sleepy town in Provence, or a major city in Melbourne.

'Alan Peat's poems stand up on the strength of his muscular language which is tough and tender in equal measures.' (Affectionate Punch)

ISBN 0 946745 46 3

£2.50 Pbk

Life's Tupperware Party

Mandy Precious

Mandy Precious' relaxed, unpretentious language conjures up beguiling images, rich in detail and analysis.

'Nothing passes Mandy Precious by – she's like a satellite dish picking up signals from all over; she puts them down too; transformed, on the page. Read and enjoy.' (Ian McMillan)

ISBN 0 946745 41 2

£2.50 Pbk

ORDER FORM

TITLE	PRICE	QTY
No Limits	£6.50	
Kiss	£5.95	
Looking for Trouble	£5.95	
Talkers Through Dream Doors	£3.50	
Crocus Five Women Poets	£5.95	
Flame	£4.50	
Art is Only a Boy's Name	£2.50	
Regrouting the Bathroom	£2.50	
Life's Tupperware Party	£2.50	
Dancing on Diamonds	£5.95	
The Delicious Lie	£4.95	
Rainbows in the Ice	£4.50	
A Matter of Fat	£4.95	
Herzone	£4.50	
Beyond Paradise	£4.50	
Relative to Me	£3.95	
Now Then	£3.50	
Black and Priceless	£3.50	
Holding Out	£3.50	

TOTAL _____

Please send a cheque or postal order, made payable to Commonword Ltd., covering the purchase price plus 50p per book postage and packing.

NAME_____

ADDRESS_____

_____

Please return to: Commonword, Cheetwood House, 21 Newton Street, Manchester M1 1FZ.